Piano
Music
for Four
Hands

Piano Music *for* Four Hands

Roger Grenier

translated & with a preface by

ALICE KAPLAN

University of Nebraska Press, Lincoln

Publication of this book was assisted by grants from the
French Ministry of Culture—National Center for the
Book and the National Endowment for the Arts.

Partita
© Editions Gallimard, 1991
Translation and preface
© 2001 by the
University of Nebraska Press
Manufactured in the United
States of America
∞

Library of Congress
Cataloging-in-Publication Data
Grenier, Roger, 1919–
[Partita. English]
Piano music for four hands / Roger Grenier ; translated
and with a preface by Alice Kaplan.
   p. cm.
ISBN 0-8032-2181-9 (cloth : alk. paper) —
ISBN 0-8032-7087-9 (pbk. : alk. paper)
1. Title: Piano music for 4 hands. II. Kaplan, Alice
Yaeger. III. Title.
PQ2613.R4323 P3513   2001
843′.914—dc21   00-064837

CONTENTS

Translator's Preface

Since the late 1940s, in over thirty books—
novels, essays, short stories—Roger Grenier has
perfected his spare, melancholy style. Closer in
his romantic irony to a Willa Cather or an F. Scott
Fitzgerald than to the experimental new novelists with
whom his generation of French writers is often identified,
he offers the American public an alternative experience of
French fiction. From the first sentence, one feels curiously
at home in his intimate, precise, and musical writing.

Piano Music for Four Hands, first published in France in
1991, is set in the southwestern French town of Pau, where
Grenier spent the greater part of his childhood and adolescence. It can be read alongside *Another November* (1986; University of Nebraska Press, 1998), one of Grenier's many Pau
chronicles. What distinguishes this novel from his others
is the centrality of music, which becomes a metaphor for
all the arts, and for the act of writing in particular. "Music
doesn't begin to cast its magic until the moment we hear
the language of our own past speaking within it," Grenier
wrote in 1979, in *Un Air de Famille.* It is this insight that he re-
fines and enlarges in the composition of *Piano Music for Four
Hands.* Michel Mailhoc, pianist, teacher, and composer,
marries his teacher's widow, has a brief career as a lounge
pianist, vacillates between two women, and finally retreats
to his country house on a hillside in the Pyrenees, where
he contemplates his failures. The bright spot in his life is
his great-niece Emma, who becomes his prize-winning student. Struggling with a fervent desire for her success and
the fear of losing her, he sends Emma into the world of
international musical stardom that he has renounced for

himself. As we follow the disparate stories that go into making Mailhoc the quizzical and disappointed man he becomes, we watch the love of music passed down from generation to generation, beginning with Michel's teacher, the Catalan genius Nicolau Arderiu, and ending with Emma, his protégée.

Michel's mentor, Arderiu, stole the hearts of many of his pupils, and Michel, both fascinated and critical of his teacher's powers, wonders if his own art of the piano is merely a means of seduction. The novel explores both his desire to seduce and his need to experience a love that goes deeper than seduction. "Piano music for four hands" can be either a seductive teaching technique or the proof of real friendship between musicians. Playing with four hands is a metaphor, both for the most profound connections art allows and for its manipulations, its easy thrills.

Though many musical compositions are evoked along the way, two composers are omnipresent in the novel. Foremost is Schubert, with his genius for the generous melody, but in whom we can always hear "the tempo of death advancing" underneath. The Schubert who interests Mailhoc —and Grenier—is finally not the "amiable composer of lieder" but "the man of the unfinished," the standard bearer for his own dissatisfaction and that of all artists. In an even darker tone is Robert Schumann, with his intellectual rigor, his suffering, and his suicidal madness.

Whatever its stylistic and tonal affinity with midcentury American literature, Roger Grenier's fictional world is tightly bound up with French history and culture. *Piano Music for Four Hands* is set against the historical tragedies of the twentieth century, drawing its characters into World War I, the Nazi occupation of France, and the Algerian War. And the novel refers back centuries earlier, evoking the legend of the Cagot people from whom the Mailhoc family is descended.

For the American reader, surely, but also for many readers in France, the story of the Cagots is the most unfamiliar one in *Piano Music for Four Hands*. Michel Mailhoc learns about his obscure heritage from historical accounts hidden in the back row of his father's bookcase. Men and women who were neither serfs nor landowners in feudal times, the Cagots of southwestern France became social pariahs, living as woodworkers, excluded from common worship, and considered lepers until as late as the seventeenth century, when they were finally rehabilitated by Louis XIV. Their condition becomes an emblem for Michel Mailhoc's own social and personal estrangement.

The story Grenier tells about World War I is a true one: On June 2, 1917, fifteen hundred men in the 370th Regiment at Coeuvres revolted after receiving orders to march on Bucy-le-Long. Thirty-two men were sentenced to death, then pardoned. A single man was executed, "to serve as an example." That man, in Grenier's fiction, is Michel Mailhoc's father, Amédée, a gentle flute player from the Pau orchestra. Descended from the accursed Cagot race, he is cursed again in his own lifetime.

Thus Michel Mailhoc, the novel's main character, loses his father before he is even born. He later loses his mentor, Nicolau Arderiu, who is taken hostage by the Nazis and deported, merely because he is a "bigwig" in Pau, and because he is known to have opposed Franco in the Spanish Civil War.

History, in *Piano Music for Four Hands,* is cruel, incontrovertible, and often absurd. History always accompanies the most private joys and sorrows, creating different melodies, which Grenier arranges for us here in a series of subtly interlocking episodes. Beneath the gentle pace of his novel is a deeply anchored fatality. "What reasons could there be for living?" Michel Mailhoc asks himself when he is still a young man: "Music, at least, offered him its charms on the journey toward nothingness."

Despite these melancholy and sorrowful airs, *Piano Music for Four Hands* resounds throughout with tenderness, humor, and longing, expressed in the simplest of terms: "Without loving and being loved," Michel Mailhoc finally decides, "we're like a fish who's been thrown up on the grass along the riverbanks."

I am grateful to the French Ministry of Culture and Communication, whose generous grant facilitated this translation. My thanks go as well to Ann Smock and Arthur Phillips for their close reading of the manuscript and to Laurel Goldman and the members of her Tuesday fiction workshop for their response to the translator's preface. Finally, I thank Roger Grenier for his participation in the work of translation and in particular for his suggestion of the title, *Piano Music for Four Hands*.

Within the translation, I have provided an occasional footnote to explain a cultural reference or a proper name unlikely to be familiar to readers of English.

We were like lanterns at

night-time parties: the pain

and the joy of several loves

consumed us.

VALERY LARBAUD, *Summer Homework*

I

The
Art
of the
Fugue

I

There was a bank of mist over the Vallée Heureuse, in the Béarn region. It glided over the hillsides. The door opened. The dog, Fresco, wandered into the garden and urinated for a long while against a sycamore tree whose leaves were already the color of autumn. Michel Mailhoc appeared in turn, wearing velour pants and a thick pullover sweater. He imitated his dog. Recently he had responded to a woman admirer who was annoying him with talk of his talent:

"If I didn't make a concert career, it's because I'd rather piss in my garden every morning."

Fresco went to sniff the scent left by his master and countersigned it by raising his leg. This show of animal friendship delighted Michel Mailhoc. He started to sing softly:

In Paris, young working girls
Are the victims of rogues . . .

A little tune from 1900 that Nicolau Arderiu used to sing, inflecting it with his thick Catalan accent.

He stopped abruptly, choked by a wave of sadness. Emma had left again after a brief visit. In Paris she must be in the midst of preparing her new tour. He hadn't asked for details, only about the tour itself: Lisbon, Milan, Vienna, Budapest, Moscow. As for the rest, she didn't tolerate questions. Those were the rules of the game. He had to make do with noticing the signs of fatigue or pain on her face, that weary gesture when she pushed back the odd white strand of hair that fell over one eye, her thinness, accentuated by her invariable black clothes, like a system of signs revealing that, from one generation to the next, we retain an innate ability to create our own unhappiness.

The mist continued to wrap around the big beech trees. The Pyrenees were invisible. They no longer existed except by an act of faith. In the same way, what was farthest from the present often escaped him. This wasn't because of any loss of memory. It had all become bizarre, alien, as if someone were telling him stories from another person's life.

That morning he had woken up in pain—his legs, his back, his sides. He lived in terror that one day the pain would reach his hands, his fingers. "Not my hands, not my hands . . ." he said to himself.

Suddenly Fresco ran toward him. He had picked up a golf ball in the grass and was showing it off with a growl, as though he both desired and refused to give it up.

"So, you've found it?" said Michel Mailhoc.

Did the golf ball give him the idea? He went to the apple tree and picked an apple. It was very round, and he squeezed it like a ball. In the old days it was thought that the Cagot people dried apples by holding them in their hands for an hour.

He had learned the family legend late. It was true that his father, Amédée, had died before he was born. I'm posthumous, Michel liked to tell himself.

There was a small library at the house in the Vallée Heureuse, doubtless assembled by Amédée, since there were books only from before 1914: *Les Misérables,* Alphonse Daudet, *L'Assommoir* and *Nana,* Edmond Rostand's plays, René Boylesve's *Lessons of Love in a Park,* books by Loti and du Farrère, Edouard Estaunié's *Things See,* Henri de Régnier's *The Double Mistress* and—it goes without saying in this house of music—Romain Rolland's *Beethoven.* The contribution of Geneviève, his mother, was limited to Raymonde Machard novels: *The Two Kisses, You Will Have a Child. . . .* As for Denis, his older brother, up until the day he left home to pursue his studies, his reading seemed not to have advanced be-

yond Jules Verne. Michel, for his part, had added only a few
poets: Baudelaire, Nerval, Laforgue, Apollinaire, and Paul-
Jean Toulet, because of how he celebrated the hillsides of
the Jurançon. But cowering behind this everyman's literature, safely hidden at the back of the glassed-in bookcase,
was a row of volumes with strange titles: *Cartulaire from Saint-
Vincent-de-Lucq, The Cagots in the Waters of Cauterets, The History
of the Accursed Races of France and Spain* by Francisque-Michel,
The Pariahs of France and Spain by Victor de Rochas, *The Cacous
of Brittany,* and several others. Michel had never paid any attention to them. After he was wounded in 1940, for want of
anything better to do, he had taken a closer look at those
books he had always left lying in the shadows of the back
row. He had understood they had to do with a caste of pariahs found especially in the Béarn region, people known as
"Crestias," "Capots," "Cagots," "Gézitains." He asked his
mother who had collected those books and why.

"It's time you knew," Geneviève responded. "We are
Cagots."

At her son's astonishment, she started to laugh, then to
cough. This was typical. A light-hearted soul, whom the
least little thing could amuse or distract, fragile lungs. It
was for Geneviève's health that, rather than live in town, the
Mailhocs had always remained on their hillside property.

"Does Denis know? He never told me about it."

"Your brother considers these stories, our big secret, idi-
otic."

His older brother didn't have much imagination. When
he called his mother and Michel "the artists," it was with
more condescension than admiration. He was a Ponts et
Chaussées engineer,* and at the time of Michel's discovery,
Denis was being held prisoner in an oflag in Pomerania.

"We are Cagots on both sides," Geneviève continued.

---

* The Ponts et Chaussées is France's most prestigious corps of engi-
neers. *Trans.*

"On your father's side, the Mailhocs, and on mine, the Caussades. We are descended from the race of Guékhazi."

"A Basque?"

"No, not at all. Guékhazi was the servant of the prophet Elijah. One day this man of God healed the Aramaic general Naaman, who had contracted leprosy. Elijah refused to accept any of the presents Naaman wanted to give him. Seeing this, Guékhazi thought it would be clever to run after the general's chariot, to catch up with him and get all the money and clothing for himself. To punish him for his cupidity, the prophet Elijah announced that the white leprosy from which he had saved Naaman would stick to Guékhazi and to his descendants, forevermore."

Geneviève Mailhoc, born a Caussade, concluded, "That is why we are sometimes called 'Gézitains.'"

Michel went to look at the Bible, where he found another story about Guékhazi. This one concerned a Sunamite lady of means who had a guest room constructed to house Elijah when he was passing through her territory. One day she complained to Elijah in front of Guékhazi. Her husband was too old, and she couldn't have children. Elijah, professional miracle maker, promised to arrange things. Of course the Bible doesn't say so, but one has the impression that this rascal Guékhazi was the instrument of providence.

Michel Mailhoc bit into the apple. It was just the way he liked them, crisp and tart. He played with the idea—it wasn't the first time—that it was his Gézitain ancestry, his Cagot heritage, that had instilled in him the feeling of always being excluded. But he knew perfectly well this wasn't so. The way he'd led his life—giving up on promises, fleeing, pursuing the eternal mirage of the woman—he alone was responsible for that. There was also perhaps the influence of Nicolau Arderiu.

He went inside to make coffee and feed the dog. On the way he couldn't help but cast a glance at the hygrometer. It was a ridiculous object, but it had always been there.

His parents had brought one back home from their honeymoon in Paris. His mother used to call it a barometer, but it was really a hygrometer in the form of a Swiss chalet, with two little people appearing in turn, one for rain, the other for sunny weather. Geneviève Mailhoc liked this object so much that when its fragile mechanism no longer worked and its little people refused to come and go, she got herself another one. She had purchased it over thirty years earlier, just before she died. This time the figurines were of two little ladies, one blue, carrying a parasol, and the other pink, carrying an umbrella. The hygrometer was nearly broken. You often had to tap it to get it to move. Michel Mailhoc confirmed what his pain had announced to him. The pink lady had come out. There was humidity in the air, and doubtless it was going to rain.

A little later, he sat at the piano and worked through the rough spots in the "Wanderer Fantasy," in particular a forte passage he had nicknamed "the cause of my insomnia."

Since its construction by some bourgeois at the beginning of the nineteenth century, the house on the hillside had been called La Paix—Peace. Yet what man, what woman can ever claim to have found peace? Michel Mailhoc had been happy or desperate, gay or jealous. Sometimes scrambling to make ends meet, sometimes enjoying good periods, but always obsessed by the irony of the name of the family property. His eyes fell on the six letters engraved on the pillar at the front gate. La Paix! And he said to himself, "La Paix! What am I waiting for to unchristen this dump!"

2

 To the oddity of his family tree, an oddity that for centuries had signified a curse, was added the memory of another event from the past, kept secret, but which was just as great a cause for exclusion. It concerned Amédée Mailhoc, Michel's father.

Amédée had married Geneviève Caussade in 1909. He was a flutist, she a violist; they both played in the Pau orchestra, which gave its concerts in the Saint-Louis Theater and the Winter Palace. It seems that, more than the mayor or the priest, it was the majestic conductor, Edouard Brunel, with his great white God-the-Father beard and his imperious baton, who had consecrated their union. Brunel, whom Henri Duparc had proclaimed "the best conductor we have in France." The love between the two musicians was born in the exchange of glances during rehearsals for Rimsky-Korsakov's *Scheherazade,* whose suave melodies made their hearts suddenly beat wildly. Soon their first son, Denis, was born. And war broke out. Amédée's military papers specified that he must report to the barracks at Charpentier in Soisson on the third day of the mobilization. In the beginning of 1917, after being slightly wounded, he was given a furlough. He did not hide from his wife the horror of the trenches and of the meaningless attacks, the growing feeling among the soldiers that their commanders kept making the same mistakes, resulting in the same massacres. When it was time to go back, to leave Geneviève and little Denis in their Vallée Heureuse, he started to cry. Geneviève was ashamed to appear more courageous than he. She didn't yet know she was pregnant with Michel, a latecomer, seven years after her first.

At the end of May, Amédée's regiment, the 370th, was at Coeuvres in the Aisne. A stray dog, a white fox terrier with a black spot on his flank, wandered through the village. Amédée fed him. A photo of the soldier survived; it shows him in a garden, in front of a wall of wisteria. He is kneeling on the ground on one knee, petting the dog, which he named Crapouillot.* One of his comrades later sent this photo to Geneviève Mailhoc. Soon the rumor circulated that the 370th was going to the front. The soldiers had had it; they started to grumble. And then the village was criss-crossed by truckloads of mutineers from the neighboring units in revolt, the 36th and 129th Infantry Regiments. On June 2, an order arrived to leave for Bucy-le-Long. Fifteen hundred men rebelled and took the road at Villers-Cotterêts with the idea of getting to Paris. They marched to cries of "Long live peace!" and "Furloughs!" Some sang the "Internationale." The gendarmerie was sent out against them in full force, then the Senegalese sharpshooters. They didn't surrender until June 5.

Thirty-two men were chosen, and a court-martial was held at the Palace of Justice in Soissons, located on the Rue du Baillon. The colonel presiding over the hearings—but was there truly a hearing on the Rue du Baillon?*—had a wart on his right cheek, and he spent his time scratching it, picking at it with his fingernail, as if he wanted to tear it off. The trial lasted four days. The overly scratched wart bled. Seventeen men were condemned to death, fifteen others to fifteen years of forced labor. The judge was unhappy. He had voted for the death sentence in each of the thirty-two cases. He dabbed at the drops of blood on his cheek with his handkerchief. The condemned men signed their requests for a pardon. Sixteen were pardoned. Only one was

---

* In military slang, a *crapouillot* was a small mortar used during the First World War to launch shells. *Trans.*
* *Baillon* in French means "bound and gagged." *Trans.*

executed, not that he was guiltier or more innocent than the others, but there had to be an example. This was Amédée Mailhoc, the man who in peacetime played the flute in an orchestra while gazing lovingly at his wife a few rows away from him. This man from the Pyrenees, whose soul had hitherto contained only the harmony of sounds and the tiered landscape of slopes, hills, blue mountains. The musician who, in his modest ambition, had composed a melody inspired by Franz Toussain's *Garden of Caresses*.

When Michel wondered why a pardon had been denied to his father only and to no one else, he could not help but think, though it was completely irrational, that he was a Cagot and that since someone had to be cursed, the choice could only have been he.

3

Geneviève Mailhoc had a strange way of remembering the war in which she had lost her husband so atrociously. For example, she used to tell Michel, "When I was bedridden during my pregnancy with you, I read Bécassine cartoons.* You can't imagine how they amused me!"

Thus the son of a man who had been executed learned he was born, not with tears, but surrounded by the Grand-Air family in their castle at Clocher-les-Bécasses. What remained of the flute player? His wife never spoke of him, nor did his eldest son. Denis was completely consumed by the family he had made himself: his wife, Yvette, his daughter, Pascale. And for Michel, who had never known him, Amédée Mailhoc was a floating shadow, like the mist on the hillside, a friendly absence, well meaning but as hypothetical as a guardian angel.

Every time they came back to the subject of 1914, Geneviève always managed to reminisce about the days when Pau was full of Englishmen, Russian princes, rich Americans, Canadians. What a happy city!

"And the evenings at Perpigna! It's a castle on the hillside in the Jurançon. It belonged to a Russian, a prince or a diplomat, I'm not sure which. Vassili Ivanovich Roukavichikov, but everyone called him Rouka. I went there three or four times to join musical soirees. The Russian, Rouka,

---

* Bécassine, J. P. Pinchon's very popular cartoon heroine from the turn of the century, was a naive little Breton maid who worked for the De Grand-Air family in a castle called "Clochers-les-Bécasses" (literally, "woodcock steeple"). *Trans.*

had composed a melody in the style of "Beth ceü de Pau" about the melancholy beauty of the Pyrenees landscape in autumn, but in French.* Every time he sang it with his accent, I could scarcely keep from laughing."

And Geneviève imitated him:

The turrrrtledoves strrreak acrrross the tenderrrrr sky
The chrrrrysanthemums drrrress up for All Saint's Day

In August, when war was declared, the crowd gathered in the evenings around the newsstand at the Place Royale, and the orchestra, which had so often soothed the splendor of summer nights with its lullabies, played the "Marseillaise," "God Save the King," and the "Brabançonne."

Soon they watched the arrival of people from the north, Parisians fleeing the German onslaught.

"The great musician Gabriel Fauré stayed with his brother Fernande, the former accreditor of schools. A little later on, during the winter of 1916–1917, his companion, the pianist Marguerite Hasselmans, came to take the cure in Pau, staying with her friend Louise Maillot. She had superb hats. But I seldom ran into her. She was too ill."

Geneviève also remembered a concert given by Francis Planté, whose playing was so romantic and whom the entire southwest considered to be the greatest pianist in the world. An old man who, out of coyness or modesty, no longer wanted to show himself in public, so he played hidden behind a curtain of green plants.

"And especially there was Cléo de Mérode. Oh! She was no longer very young. She must have been thirty-four, thirty-five years old. But she was the most beautiful woman I have ever seen. She had rented an apartment on the Boulevard des Pyrénées. I used to see her often in the neighborhood church, Saint-Martin's, praying. She had retired from

* "Beth ceü de Pau" is a well-known song in Béarn dialect. *Trans.*

dancing. But she took part in a gala at the Saint-Louis Theater, a benefit for the wounded. She wore a dress made of pale blue taffeta. I was in the orchestra. She also came to the Winter Palace for another charity ball. In navy blue this time, she danced the one-step. It was a novelty. Her partner was a splendid man! One heard a lot of stories about her in Paris. They gossiped about the King of Belgium, Léopold II: Cléo and Cléopold. But in our town, she was received in the highest society. She was so proper! And her profile so delicate, I'd almost say virginal! And her mouth! If I were a man, I would have adored her mouth! And then when the war was over, she left us. She went back up to Paris." To judge from Geneviève's stories, she apparently was never subjected to the opprobrium of being the wife of a man executed for mutiny. Perhaps she had managed to hide it and to pass herself off as a war widow like the others. The tradition of the Cagots, long accustomed to hiding their secret, their curse, may have helped her. But it wasn't clear. It seemed that in the eyes of Geneviève, being descended from the Cagots was only one piece of the family folklore.

Leafing through the books in the library at La Paix, Michel learned that *cagot* is a Béarn word meaning "white leper" and may have been derived from *caas Goths,* Goth dogs. According to popular belief, the Cagots are descended from lepers whose distant ancestor was Guékhazi, or from the Visigoths, the Saracens, the Jews, the Albigensians, or perhaps even the Christians from Spain who had collaborated with Charlemagne. Recent work has shown these theories to be pure fantasy. The Crestias or Cagots were in fact the products of the very archaic feudal situation, of social structures in the foothills of the Pyrenees passed down from the high Middle Ages. As in many other parts of the world, these structures led to the formation of a caste. But the legend remains stronger than the truth.

The caste of Cagots, these people who owned no land, was kept at a distance, condemned to work with wood as carpenters and required to live far away from the parish community. They were forced to attend mass separately and even to enter the church by a special door, a low door. Untouchables.

Was the Visigoth queen Pedauque related to the Cagots? In the langue d'oc language spoken in the southwest of France during the Middle Ages, *Pé d'auque* meant goose foot. The queen had webbed feet. And the Cagots were required to carry a mark of their infamy, a red mark in the form of a goose or duck claw.

In the library there was a medievalesque novel by Madame de Montpezat, the kind produced in the Romantic era, *Corisande de Mauléon*. In it, Michel found a superb tirade:

> The Cagots! Objects of horror, marked on their
> shoulders by a cloth in the form of a goose foot, to
> be recognized and avoided like snakes, except they
> let themselves be smashed without defending them-
> selves! . . . the Cagots who, under threat of death, had
> to promise not to dirty the soil on which they walked
> with their bare feet! . . . the Cagots, expelled to the
> forest to work as woodcutters, an occupation made
> infamous on account of them! . . . the Cagots, not
> included in the charity advocated by the Gospel,
> excluded from the assemblies of Christians, separated
> from them in church by a wall, entering by another
> door, ending up far from everyone in a cemetery all
> to themselves! . . .

As early as the reign of Henri IV, medical commissions examined the Cagots and declared that they were not ill. Louis XIV abolished their separate status in the name of liberty, which "has always been the policy of this realm," and of equality among his subjects. In the eighteenth century, the parliament in Bordeaux, of which Montesquieu was a member, severely reprimanded acts of violence against the Cagots on several occasions. Still, despite these efforts by kings and by the highest authorities, it wasn't until the end of the eighteenth and the beginning of the nineteenth century that the so-called hereditary lepers melted into the mass of the population. But like the Marranos, Jews forcibly converted by the Spanish Inquisition, they kept the secret of their origins in the bosom of their families. From generation to generation, they recounted the history of their segregation, the distant memory of the time when in the Valley of the Béarn they were forbidden to dance with the other villagers.

4

When the Second World War broke out, what had struck Geneviève, and what she never tired of retelling, was that in September 1939 the radio station had opened its studio to the pianist Alfred Cortot, thanks to whom one could hear the music of Chopin day after day, as if such a riposte would be enough to stop the tanks that were crushing Poland. Soon it was time for the "Funeral March."

Geneviève Mailhoc had also found a cliché she liked repeating: "The First World War took my husband, and now the second one is taking my sons!"

Denis had been drafted as an officer in the engineering corps. Michel, who had been exempted as a student and who hadn't yet completed his military service, was incorporated—no one knew why—into the colonial infantry reserve at Mont-de-Marsan, decked out in a uniform with red navy anchors, rapidly trained, and sent to the war zone. ("How can someone be sent to a regiment of the colonial infantry without every having set foot in the colonies?" Geneviève asked). But finally, after June 1940, with one of them a prisoner and the other one wounded, their ordeal had ended, more or less.

Once again the city was invaded by refugees. But this time was less gay. Those who were fleeing knew their lives were in immediate danger. The south of France was only a stop along the way. Many tried to cross the Pyrenees. Even in the Pyrenees region, there was an internment camp with a sinister reputation. The misery of the Jews, who were forced to flee and hide, was a reminder, only much worse, of the ancestral history when discrimination had struck the Gézitains. In her conversation, Geneviève no longer exhibited the insouciance, the nonchalance that had been her style during the First World War. Suddenly she found she had aged.

The tribulations of wartime did not spare ordinary families, scattering and regrouping them like flakes of snow left to the wind's fancy. Geneviève was joined at her house in the Vallée Heureuse by her son Michel, recovering with difficulty from his wounds, and also by her daughter-in-law Yvette and little Pascale, Yvette's six-year-old child. Denis's wife had decided to stay put until the prisoner's return.

The exodus also brought to the Béarn a personage who had once figured among the region's celebrities and who had played a great role in the life of Michel Mailhoc and doubtless also that of Geneviève: the pianist Nicolau Arderiu.

5

 His story takes us back to the end of the First World War. A flamboyant impresario named La Flèche, whose enterprises long monopolized the local news, had the idea of opening a roller-skating rink. Not far from the place where the exquisite Cléo had lived so discreetly, you could now hear the constant grinding of metal wheels as they rolled along the cement tracks, an empty sound that echoed from the walls, the floor, and the ceiling. The citizens of Pau were not long enchanted by roller-skating. Soon the rink closed. In its place someone installed a tea salon, which tried to be original by offering a bookstore, an exhibit hall, a conference room, and concerts, all in the same spot. It was called "The Pastime." It was there that Nicolau Arderiu came to sit at the piano stool. He had to turn its crank to lower it quite a bit, since he was of an imposing stature. For a public that must have included a few connoisseurs, he played the Fourth French Suite in E-flat Major BWV 815, the *Waldstein* Sonata, Debussy's *Goldfish,* and finally the *Feuilles d'album* by the great Basque composer Albeniz.

Soon it was known that at the age of fourteen, Nicolau Arderiu had had the immense honor of playing a two-piano duet with Albeniz. Arderiu himself was of Catalan descent. His father had been director of the Barcelona Conservatory. His grandfather, a well-known pianist, had worked with Zimmermann in Paris and with Franz Liszt in Lyons and had counted Granados among his many students. Nicolau Arderiu loved Granados as well, both the man and his music. He couldn't get over his senseless death in the torpedoing of the *Sussex* in 1916 at Pas-de-Calais. But above all he admired the pianist Ricardo Vines for the way he played Schumann's Fantasia op. 17.

There are two types of musicians: those who wear their hair long in back, falling on their shoulders, and those whose rebellious frizzy locks form a crown. Nicolau Arderiu was a hybrid, because his hair was frizzy, and no matter what he did, pieces of it stuck out on each side horizontally. He was proud to be a Catalan, but he liked to declare, "I am a Carthaginian." Isn't the Punic family of the Barca credited with having founded Barcelona?

Since the age of nineteen, Arderiu had been a highly respected piano teacher. He also gave recitals, but rarely, for his stage fright had reached the level of a disability. One evening as he was playing Beethoven's Sonata 18 in B-flat for Piano, he was so flustered he forgot the minuetto. So there he was, launched directly into the scherzo of the presto con fuoco, which he dispatched in the most brilliant manner possible. When he came back to his senses and noticed his mistake, all he could do was repeat a terrible Catalan curse: "Fabe da Deu! Fabe da Deu! . . . The minuetto!" Because of his stage fright, he always began his concerts with a slow piece.

How had he come there? Why had he made this double migration, not only from the south to the north of the Pyrenees but from the east to the west? His burgeoning career as a piano teacher had barely started when his seductive power over women got the better of him. Students threw themselves at him. He couldn't resist. His large pianist's hands embraced them. This made for some trouble. It is said— and he would say so himself— that it's better to be prudent; nonetheless, he was weak. Naive too. Elisabeth Förster said of Nietzsche, "He was so myopic, he couldn't see the comedy of faces." Arderiu wasn't myopic; his innocence made him blind. Throughout his life, he was a Don Juan who made no effort to seduce but didn't know how to say no.

Thus he thought he had conquered Francesca Navarro,

who had done her utmost to be conquered. Francesca's father was the director of the Teatro del Liceo, the prestigious opera that Barcelona high society had built as a temple to its own glory. The lovers had taken, or thought they had taken, many precautions in the vain hope that their affair would remain a secret. Soon they were unmasked. At the Liceo, where a third of the seats were the hereditary property of the city's leading families, no one had known such panic since the anarchist attack that had resulted in twenty deaths inside the theater in 1892. The scandal wouldn't be matched until the evening when, in the presence of King Alphonse XIII, the audience at the Liceo gave a standing ovation to Pablo Casals, shouting, "He is our king!" Nicolau was at the height of his love, at that moment when one believes that this time passion will be eternal. He fled with Francesca. They crossed the border and, after wandering for a while in France, settled in Brussels. This was in February 1914. "We won't stay here," the Barcelonans kept repeating. "We can't take the cold." But when they didn't stay in Belgium, it wasn't because of the bitter cold. It was the war that drove them out. In the destiny of the musician Nicolau Arderiu, this would be only the first such occasion. As if his own personal follies weren't enough, he had more than his share of being disrupted and condemned to wander by history. Until the final tribulation, which was tragic.

Michel Mailhoc, for whom Nicolau was a master, a model, never ceased to marvel at being, at least on this score, totally different from him. He wondered why in his own case, after a few half-hearted attempts at escape, he had become sedentary, practically never leaving La Paix, the house in the Vallée Heureuse.

Francesca and Nicolau tried to set up house in Paris, then in Rouen, where they were married. They left Normandy for Bordeaux, then went north to Nantes. Finally, in the Loire Valley, the pianist started to earn a decent living, thanks to students and a few concerts. To be accepted as a foreigner in this period, when the war was inciting the French to nativism, he never missed a chance to lend a hand for benefit concerts, no matter how mediocre. The Spanish were not well thought of, and the fact that he was Catalan didn't matter; no one could tell the difference. Those were the days when King Alphonse XIII used to sigh, "All that's left of the francophiles are the riffraff and me."

The war had scarcely ended when Francesca fell ill. The doctors recommended the climate in the Béarn or the Basque country. So they came to Pau, and still she didn't improve. She assumed the role of the fragile, permanently lethargic woman. Nicolau Arderiu began once again to succumb to his pretty students and even to the less pretty.

If up until now, the exiled musician had struggled, it must be said to the credit of the Béarnais people that his merits were immediately recognized. Almost as soon as he gave his first concert, in the former skating rink. In Pau for quite some time, the art of song had been the domain of maestro Albert Torf, conductor of operettas and operas at the Winter Palace. But he lacked a soloist, a virtuoso face-to-face with a big black piano on concert evenings, like a matador confronting his bull at five in the afternoon. Nicolau Arderiu's unusual silhouette, his great height, his accent, contributed as much as his art to his reputation not only as a remarkable pianist but also as a peerless teacher. Soon he accepted only advanced students. "No children, no beginners," he used to say. He also gave lessons at the two American schools in which the city took great pride, Park Lodge School for boys and York House for girls, and this only increased his glory.

The boys and girls were received in his home (perhaps one should say girls, since they far outnumbered the boys) in an old-fashioned parlor, as if their teacher had always lived there and had even inherited this home from his parents or grandparents. The color of the wallpaper, the armchairs, the curtains seemed faded. All that shined were the black

Pleyel piano and the leaves of a philodendron, trimmed to the shape of a hand and fingers. When Arderiu got angry, he would shake one of the leaves and yell, "Look! This plant could play the piano better than you do!"

Often while the student worked, he paced up and down the parlor; then brusquely approaching them from behind, he would seize their forearms to correct their position.

He insisted as well on the position of the thumb. Then sitting next to them, guiding the right hand while playing the same thing an octave higher, he shaped their playing little by little, bringing to it infinitesimal nuances.

"You couldn't write these notes any better, but you can always play them better."

His conclusion was always the same: "Natural! . . . Natural!"

Easy to say. In the piece played by the student, no note was missing, but it made no sense. When it was Arderiu's turn, he sat down at the piano and by playing "naturally" illuminated the composer's ideas.

"Each note is an atom, a drop of water, a world in and of itself, and yet their juxtaposition not only creates a language, tells a story, but also gives birth to an emotion. Try to understand this! . . . Actually, it is like the human voice! The great model is the human voice. As Chopin used to say, you aren't playing the piano, you are playing music!"

Congenitally romantic, he did not like those composers who, though perhaps very strong in technique and knowledge, did not move him. He dispatched them with the help of a quotation: "As Goethe said, 'To me that's just noise.'"

He illustrated his lessons with anecdotes, stories:

"Franz Liszt was an aristocrat. At least he thought he was. Don't play him like a Neapolitan ditty!"

Arderiu's favorite joke concerning the composer of *Etudes of Transcendental Execution* was to cry out, "You're just like Ghiza Zichy! . . . You don't know who Ghiza Zichy was? . . . A student of Liszt's. . . . Do you know why I'm comparing you to Ghiza Zichy?"

"No, sir."

"He had one arm!"

A large folding screen, an English thing covered with scraps, divided the parlor in two. Arderiu must have found it in some antique shop after the death of one of those old British spinsters who were left behind when their compatriots abandoned the Béarn. The region had known them in their youth, and now they were expiring, one after the other. During his lessons, as if she were hiding, the long-suffering Francesca frequently stood behind the screen, whose pasted-on forms were peeling off. On one of them, a brave fisherman played the violin in front of a house made of an upside-down boat, and two children, boys, danced to the sound of his music. Did Francesca stand there because she was jealous? It was not at all clear.

Still, Nicolau had to keep on his guard. He had composed a little sonata for one of his female students, and it was one of his most successful pieces for piano. Though he never knew how, Francesca got wind of the fact that the sonata had been inspired by a girl. He realized soon enough she could not tolerate his playing it in her presence, nor could he put it on the program of any of his recitals. She had decreed that the sonata was a failure.

6

Francesca might have been better advised to be suspicious of Geneviève Mailhoc, among others. Didn't popular belief hold that women of the Cagot race were ardent pleasure seekers? She had gotten to know Arderiu because all the musicians in the city met one another sooner or later. There weren't that many of them. During a concert, just after she had performed alone on the viola in Vieuxtemps's *Capriccio,* Arderiu paid her an extraordinary compliment. He declared that she played the viola the way a great opera singer might sing. When Michel was five, the Catalan maestro suddenly proposed, "It's time to make a pianist of him. Let me take him on."

His offer, almost an order, was even more surprising since it contradicted his motto, "No children, no beginners." Perhaps Arderiu wanted to please the young widow and found a way to see her frequently. Of course, he refused to be paid. You don't take money from a colleague who, what's more, lost her husband in the war. Soon he proclaimed he had never seen such a talented beginner.

"This child will be my equal. Or nearly."

He taught him how to play Gabriel Fauré's *Dolly* along with him—it was a piece for four hands. Sharing the keyboard, conversing in music with Nicolau Arderiu was, in the child's eyes, an unbelievable privilege. At the same time, it troubled him that his mentor predicted such a glorious future for him. He wondered what would happen if the musician were right, if he were more intelligent or at least more artistic than ordinary mortals, and the thought made him unhappy. He considered himself just like other people, ordinary, and he preferred it that way. He was only ten when he learned his father had been executed for mutiny in 1917. Executed as an example, as they used to say. This distinction, this weighty family secret gave him the desire to be like everyone else. At that time he was still unaware his ancestors were Cagots. And as if the old curse had left a genetic trace, the feeling of being unworthy overwhelmed him anytime he thought about himself. Basically, he didn't like himself. Later he would constantly oscillate between the desire to be a well-known musician and the need for obscurity. He always drifted between the two, dissatisfied with himself and seen by others as something of a ne'er-do-well.

While he wanted to be like everybody else, he never stopped asking himself what reasons there could be for living if you were like everybody else. We are born with no other goal than to die. Do we march toward death in the same lockstep as the herd? Music, at least, offered him its charms on the journey toward nothingness. At the age of fourteen, Schubert was already inflecting his Quartet in B-flat Major with the muffled hammering that runs through his most serious works, the tempo of death advancing. Schubert . . . In 1928 for the centenary of the composer's death, Nicolau Arderiu organized a Schubertiade. He didn't want this evening to take place at the Saint-Louis Theater or at the Winter Palace but in a more intimate spot, Pétron Hall, named after a vendor of musical instruments. Just as with all of his public appearances, Arderiu was overcome with stage fright. He groaned. "I'm incapable of walking. I have no more legs. If you want me there at all costs, get me a stretcher!"

They had to prop him up all the way to the concert hall. Such a case isn't unusual. Many great pianists are stricken with this kind of stage fright. They turn to mush before going on stage. When her time came, Emma would drip with an anxious sweat before every concert. All the same, Arderiu was close to exceeding the limit. To excuse his weakness, he recalled that Brahms, during the premiere of his violin concerto, was so unnerved he forgot to put on his suspenders. His shirttail slipped out of his trousers, which greatly distracted the audience, and as a result, his dear friend, the violinist Joseph Joachim, nearly botched his solo.

The evening began with mixed choirs singing "Hymn to the Eternal," "God during the Storm," and "God, Creator of the World." Next came Michel's turn because Nicolau Arderiu had absolutely insisted that his young student, barely eleven, take part in the Schubert celebration. Unlike his mentor, Michel felt so calm he was alarmed, thinking he was abnormal. He played an Impromptu in F Minor from op. 142.

Without taking his student's age into consideration— and this was typical of Arderiu's lack of logic—he gave Michel this peremptory piece of advice: "Remember what Nietzsche said: the pianist who performs the work of a master will have played his best if he has made people forget the master and given the illusion that he has just related an event from his own life or that he has just experienced a great moment."

How could an eleven-year-old boy take in the incredible blend of whimsy and sorrow interlaced in this impromptu? When a student's interpretation of a piece seemed drab to him, didn't Arderiu bark, "You know nothing about life!"

The public, who didn't expect nearly as much, applauded the pianist's youth. Nicolau Arderiu climbed onto the stage to embrace him. Then he took the floor. Both excited and half-paralyzed with emotion, he declared almost in a shout:

"There are musicians—I could cite them, I could name them—who see nothing in Schubert but an amiable composer of lieder. Thus they do not understand that his music is intensely dramatic! The depth, the variety, the multiplicity of his means of expression are without limits! His sonatas are the sites of conflict, drama, theatrical surprises, and each time we hear them, our astonishment and admiration take our breath away! Here is his posthumous Sonata in C Minor."

He sat down at the piano and played so that the audience wept. With his own throat knotted, he could barely introduce the musician who came after him, the mezzo-soprano, Lydia Lafforgue. Tall, her face forming a perfect oval that emphasized the neat shape of her heavy ash blonde hair held back in a chignon—which, in that era of bobs, made for an old-fashioned effect—she was not without beauty, but it was the beauty of another era. Her parents had taken refuge in Pau after a reversal of fortune. Lydia Lafforgue and her mother ran a candy shop near the château of Henri IV. The young woman never recovered from being prevented by her family's prejudices from entering the conservatory. And now, she thought bitterly, ruin had come all the same. A candy store! A business!

Announcing the singer, Nicolau confided to the audience in his thick foreign accent, "Now we should all be as in Musset's poem, *The Willow*. 'Suddenly there was the deepest silence / When Georgina Smolen got up to sing . . .'"

He sat down at the piano and accompanied the mezzo-soprano in "Gretchen at the Spinning Wheel" and "The Elf-king." Next, with the additional accompaniment of a clarinetist, she sang "The Shepherd on the Rock."

Despite the success of this Schubertiade, Lydia Lafforgue was never again heard singing in any of the concerts organized by Nicolau Arderiu. Francesca, so often betrayed without knowing it or without complaining, had now fixated her jealousy on this person who, despite her dutiful and nearly outmoded appearance, was said to be loose.

7

Arderiu often showed up at La Paix without advance notice, or rather they were warned at the last minute by his motorcycle backfiring loudly on the hillside. Then Geneviève would blush, look herself over in the mirror, and start rearranging the knickknacks, suddenly finding them out of place. Ever flamboyant, the musician would prop his cycle on its kickstand, proclaiming, "I am the centaur Chiron, coming to see his student Achilles."

Even if it were true that Chiron taught young Achilles to play the pipes, Michel felt no calling as a warrior, and Arderiu was far from deserving the reputation for wisdom that the king of the centaurs had enjoyed.

At other times his arrival was silent, for he loved to exercise and walk the four miles separating the city from their property. Then he would arm himself with a cane and a large Panama hat, which gave him a vaguely old-fashioned silhouette and made him look like Wagner in a Romantic etching. And doubtless the Catalan pianist also happened to show up at the house when he knew his student wouldn't be there.

Michel feared, loved, and detested this excessive teacher. In short, with the passing days Arderiu became a father.

Since he had learned that Amédée Mailhoc had met his end tied to a post with six men standing a few steps away and six others kneeling behind, all aiming at him, drawing a bead on his heart (Was he blindfolded? Was he still breathing when the officer fired the coup de grâce to his head?), Michel sought out stories about mutineers. One in particular stuck with him. In a village on the front, four condemned men were to go before the firing squad. They weren't to be executed together but rather one after the other. Three had already received their twelve bullets. Two gendarmes surrounded the fourth man to take him to his punishment. At that very moment a mortar shell exploded, spreading panic and killing the two gendarmes. The condemned man was only slightly wounded. He took advantage of the situation to flee. He was never found. After the war it was learned he had managed to reach Spain. In his dreams, Michel Mailhoc imagined that the fugitive was his father and that he had returned from Spain under the identity of Nicolau Arderiu. He also imagined in his most secret thoughts that Francesca, the eternal invalid, would end up dying and that Arderiu would marry Geneviève. But just as had happened with his real father, the man executed in 1917, Nicolau Arderiu vanished in an instant.

The boy had just turned fifteen, and his teacher had nearly kept his promise to make a great pianist of him. Michel had already begun to appear in concerts. But one day when he went for his lesson, he found a locked door.

In town the scandal was enormous. For the second time in his life, Arderiu had fled, carrying off one of his students. Florence Palmade was barely eighteen. In other words, she was born the year the musician had left Barcelona in the company of Francesca Navarro! She was the daughter of an important businessman, a member of the city council. This young lady had nevertheless been educated as a boarder in the severe and pious school attached to the Ursuline convent. But who looking at this brunette, at her matte skin, her full lips, her very black eyes with their mauve lids, would have thought of the Ursulines? Poor Francesca, whom despair seemed to have brought to the gates of death, had been taken in by friends. Geneviève showed little sorrow, only annoyance. She wondered what would become of her son's musical studies. Either she knew how to conceal her feelings, or her affair with Arderiu had cooled off, or else her lighthearted nature, which made her talk about Cléo de Mérode while her husband was being executed or about Bécassine cartoons when she was about to give birth, made her incapable of great sorrows. One day long afterward when the Catalan pianist's name came up, she told her son, "He was crazy about me."

A brazen confession that shocked Michel.

The disappearance of his mentor prompted the young man to compete for admission to the Paris Conservatory. I'm going too, he told himself. I'm leaving my town. His heart was heavy.

8

 James Warner and his sister Daisy were students at the American schools, Park Lodge and York House. They took classes from Nicolau Arderiu there and also private lessons at his house. They seemed to have wandered the world before their mother set up house at the foot of the Pyrenees. They never spoke of their father except to complain when his alimony payment was late. In a way, they too were a bit like orphans. There was a touch of the bohemian in them, which attracted Michel. They had met at their piano teacher's. Michel and James were the same age. Together, they could never get enough of poking around the countryside on their bikes. Despite the rather steep hills, the bike was really Michel's only form of transportation to school or to his music lessons. James was trying his hand at playing jazz, and he gave Michel a taste for it. If Arderiu had heard them, would he have been horrified? Not necessarily. One day he had proclaimed, "Naturally, classical music transports you, moves you to tears. But a simple tango can make your heart spin. Ah, the tango!"

After the disappearance of their teacher, although they no longer met each other in his parlor with its faded colors, between the Pleyel, the folding screen, and the philodendron, their friendship didn't come to an end.

Daisy was three years older than the boys. She was tall, slim, with beautiful hair, a large, slightly savage mouth, the opposite of the little Kewpie doll mouths that would remain in vogue for a bit longer. She generally wore light dresses, cut straight, with an unbuttoned cardigan over them and a belt knotted any which way. Flat shoes, bobby socks. In short, Michel, who was going through puberty, had eyes only for this American girl. James, who had little regard for his sister, took a piece of paper and pencil one day and drew for his friend the form of her breasts, which he found too soft, already sagging.

James was only studying the piano as an amateur. "What do you want to do with yourself later?" Michel asked him. The American didn't know.

"I don't believe in the Frenchman Descartes's cogito. I have so little sense of existing. And when I'm alone, none at all."

When pushed however, he did admit that he would like to devote himself to theater and ballet. But one shouldn't dream.

Then Michel left Pau. He saw the Americans a few more times when vacation brought him back home. In 1935 the Warners went back to the United States. They exchanged a few letters and that was the end of it. Daisy's letters, actually, were disappointingly trite. She complained about her studies at the university, about her stepfather (so there was a stepfather?), about being bored. She was already forgetting her French and made numerous mistakes. One day in 1938 he received the announcement of Daisy's marriage to a certain Tom Holmes, without a personal note. He wondered if he should send a gift and finally settled on a congratulatory card.

Yet he nursed a tenderness for these vanished friends. James was a fine fellow, very intelligent in his way, and Michel could still picture the tall, delicate Daisy, with a face like the pretty girls in Hollywood movies.

9

 When one left La Paix and crossed the road, there was a small wood that went down in a straight slope to the bottom of a hill. Each time he saw this wood, which is to say every day, he remembered the long wooded slope, "somewhere in France" as the saying went in 1940 — somewhere and more precisely on the banks of the Loire. It was on this slope, in a procession of wounded men, infantry from his regiment, that he had made his retreat. He dragged himself along with a limp, blinded by the blood streaming from a gash in his scalp, with a numb leg that seemed crushed, making him wonder if it still existed. And on the incline of that little woods, he had suddenly found himself back in his childhood when he would wander across the road to cavort among the trees, all the way to the bottom of the hill, where he actually played war games, suddenly spreading his arms in a cross, hit by an imaginary bullet, lifeless among the rotting leaves. He was fond of that word, "lifeless." But in June 1940 on the banks of the Loire, he was no longer playing. Other wounded men came down across the woods, holding on to each other, screaming in pain when they stumbled. A few rare stretchers carried some of them. He had crawled, slid, rolled until he was exhausted, as if the only thing that mattered from then on was to get down that hill. At the beginning of the war, he was surprised to find himself part of the French army that had assassinated his father. And today he and the French army were smashed to pieces. He fainted. Then he came to on a stretcher, lying on the floor of a village church — a makeshift hospital. And from then on, the slope of the woods on the other side of the road took him back to the wars of childhood and from childhood to that wood with its new leaves shattered by gunfire, near the Loire.

He also saw in passing a little girl who used to pick chestnuts in autumn. And more recently he had added yet another association. As he stood in the little woods in front of the trees climbing up the hillside as if to imitate the rise of a Gothic cathedral in their effort to pull themselves up from the ground and reach the sky, he thought of Bruckner's Seventh Symphony, so religious but even more sublime when it spoke simply of our own world here below, with its great waves of feeling that carried you further and further, toward what abyss? And he wondered if, at measure 177, it was better to strike the cymbal or to omit it. Bruckner, hesitating, had crossed it out. In 1940 the woods had echoed with a metallic din, and the cymbal would have been very suitable. But what could the little wood of the Vallée Heureuse, with its bird songs, have to do with a crashing cymbal?

10

After he ran off with Florence Palmade, Nicolau Arderiu's first stop was Barcelona. But his return to his native city was a disappointment. No one was interested in the prodigal son. He had the impression that the musicians of the Catalan capital weren't willing to squeeze together even a little to make room for him. He barely managed to get a few radio jobs. The fugitives decided to leave once again and settle in Alicante. There the pianist soon found students. He didn't make a fortune, but the city was pleasant with its ocean, its palm trees along tiled sidewalks whose patterns imitated waves. Arderiu was surprised in returning to Spain to find he saw it as a foreigner, with an eye for the exotic. Before he never would have noticed the women wrapped in their Manila shawls, the beauty of the morning sky, the rough seas. The adolescents to whom he gave piano lessons were named Lola, Pepita, Carmen, Charo, Mercedes, Aracelli, Concha, Manola. Their names intoxicated him. Then came 1936.

Did they have to flee again? Arderiu felt too old to go to war. But he had chosen sides. He detested Franco, his Moroccan soldiers, and his priests with all his might. The old Catalan anarchist, who had been dormant within him, woke up again. Alicante happened to be located in the last Republican bastion, so he and Florence managed to survive there to the bitter end. Beautiful students were rare. The bourgeois families had fled, and the others, who, openly or not, tended to side with the Fascists, didn't want anything to do with this piano teacher who was a friend of the Frente Crapular. It meant near poverty.

On March 30, 1939, the Italian General Gambara made his entry into the port, which was flooded with thousands of refugees. Arderiu and his companion managed to get passage on an English ship.

They settled in Paris, or rather they thought they had settled there. The events of June 1940 threw them out on the roads again. Caught up in the flow of panicked civilians and wandering soldiers, fired on by airplanes, they crossed the Loire not far from the spot where Michel would be wounded the very next day in one of the last skirmishes of the war, a local battle over nothing—not exactly over nothing, it was a question of honor. It was at the end of that flight that the flamboyant pianist and his brown-haired companion came back to Pau.

In the meantime, the ill-fated Francesca had died, and Arderiu and Florence had married. They realized that the city was not unwelcoming, and they could stay there.

War forces you to make do with uncertainty. Michel wondered what he would do when he went back to civilian life. With France occupied, there was no question of his returning to Paris and perhaps starting a concert career there. He would stay in Pau and try to find students. This plan bumped up against a practical difficulty. Who would come all the way to the Vallée Heureuse, when cars were so rare and not many people had legs sturdy enough to climb the hills by bike? Everything was scarce. How will we stay warm? Geneviève said. But immediately his mind, like a bird letting itself drift in the wind, recalled the coal vendors from before the war—the other one, the Great War. They delivered their coal sacks in wagons drawn by oxen. The backs of the oxen were covered with a lovely Basque cloth to protect them from the flies, a cloth that stayed clean despite the coal.

Michel thought he might apply for a job at the local music school. But he received a phone call, and he recognized the coppery voice, the thick accent of his former teacher.

Arderiu had learned he had been wounded and was worried about him.

For the time being, the Catalan musician was staying in a little furnished flat behind the Palais de Justice. When he welcomed Michel on his first visit, he hesitated a moment, as if he didn't know quite how he was going to play his part, if it would be piano or forte. His natural proclivity carried the day. He started out fortissimo. "My life is a scherzo, a joke, buffoonery!"

He crossed the room in three long strides, then back again. His long frizzy locks, still sticking out on each side, had whitened.

" 'Take me away!' That's what she told me."

Figuring that he had now apologized sufficiently for the past, for his having run away and abandoned his disciple, Arderiu opened his arms in a theatrical gesture and hugged Michel. At that moment the young man knew he couldn't bear a grudge against the man who for eight years had failed him. Arderiu was still his teacher and his mentor.

"When I was young," the Catalan said, "I envied the monks of Montserrat. I dreamed of being one of them, of devoting myself in solitude to restoring ancient musical scores. . . . Fate decided otherwise!"

Michel didn't doubt that what Arderiu was telling him was sincere, but he had trouble imagining him in a monastic cell, far from the world and from women.

"I'm fifty years old, and I'm back at square one."

Arderiu was off and running: "What is important in music, in studying, in suffering too — and I don't exclude suffering in love — is never to forget that our supreme goal is wisdom! What are your plans?"

Michel told him of his uncertainties.

"You know what we'll do?" the musician decided, as if struck with a sudden inspiration. "I've been offered a large villa near Beaumont Park. It's a bit dilapidated, abandoned. The rent is negligible. We'll start a school, the two of us.

And a concert series. It's wartime. There's no entertainment; people are bored and they need to lift their spirits."

At that point, Arderiu didn't even have a piano. But some of his admirers would soon lend him one.

The front door opened. Florence appeared. The woman whom Michel held responsible for what had happened to him because of Nicolau Arderiu's flight. She seemed so pretty, so young, his hostility dissolved immediately. It was her eyes especially, with their mauve lids.

"But when this damned war is over," Nicolau Arderiu said, "you have to return to Paris. A great career awaits you."

Michel looked at Florence, and suddenly he no longer wanted to leave.

"Don't you recognize me?" the young woman said. "I can place you very clearly. We met several times when we went to take lessons in this man's home."

"I'm embarrassed, more than embarrassed—I'm ashamed. I never recognize anyone. I'm not good at remembering faces. But yours, I should have remembered."

"You were barely a teenager. You must have had other things on your mind."

"I shouldn't have."

He mentally calculated: I was fifteen and she was eighteen. Exactly the same age as Daisy Warner. That was in 1932. Today she is twenty-six and Nicolau Arderiu is fifty! It's not possible.

II

Michel was half way through César Franck's Prelude, Aria, and Finale when Nicolau Arderiu made his entry. The pianist broke off his playing.

"How good of you to stop with that Gothic music," proclaimed Arderiu in his most thunderous voice. "He's punch drunk on chromatic intervals. Clearly I'm no more of a Franckiste: *c-k,* than a Franquiste: *q-u-i!* Enchanted by his own pun,* he made one concession. "Fortunately, from the *Beatitudes* to his Quintet, he came down from heaven to earth. You see, he had fallen in love! That I can understand. By the way, in Paris didn't you have a girlfriend?"

"Yes," Michel responded. "There was a woman, Muriel."

An image came to him suddenly, so precise it made him grow quiet, of the day they were in bed for the last time in her room on the Rue de Vaugirard, Muriel's long brown body united with his, her on top, as she liked.

He spoke again in a different tone of voice. "When I was drafted, we didn't say 'good-bye for now'; we said our adieus. We felt very strongly that a world was ending, that everything we had known belonged to the past. Our relationship too. As though the spider's web had broken."

"The spider's web?"

"In a manner of speaking."

In the letters she had sent him in Paris, Michel's mother urged him to visit a former friend of hers, "a very interesting man, a poet." She had known him years earlier in Pau, where he had gone to treat early-stage tuberculo-

---

* The French called the supporters of Franco, "Franquistes." *Trans.*

sis. "He can introduce you to the world of artists," Gene-viève claimed, sounding calculating for once. One lonely day, Michel ended up calling him. At the conservatory he had barely made any friends. There was always, justified or not, that feeling of being excluded. He thought they were making fun of his southwestern accent.

The poet was a voluble character, who gesticulated in a manner just short of ridiculousness, but he welcomed the student warmly. He kept him until his wife, a professor of geography, arrived. As for him, his status as poet and invalid exempted him from having a job. As Michel was about to leave, he suggested another get-together.

"Since you are a pianist, I will introduce you to one of the greatest. He accepts visitors every Thursday."

With his poet to guide him, Michel thus found himself in a salon on the Rue de Rome, crowded with thirty or more people. There were other poets, musicians, society men and women, a priest, young people. The maestro was a fat man with a pale face, his bald forehead dominating a crown of long hair. There was a light layer of lipstick on his mouth. With a touch of white on his face and a red nose, he would have been a musical clown.

Michel had received the following information from his guide:

"His lover is the policeman with the long mustache, who is usually on guard in front of the Saint-Lazare train station at the corner of the Rue du Havre."

Someone called for silence. The musical clown sat down at his piano. He played only Chopin and it was on Chopin that his fame rested, but he played him like no one else. Until that day, Michel hadn't much liked Chopin. And suddenly, watching the clown's fingers run along the keyboard with this tempo rubato, this irregularity, he understood what Chopin was saying, and he wanted to play himself so that through his own fingers, this music would speak to him and confide its secrets in him.

When the pianist had finished, people crowded around him to clasp his hands, hug him, as if they wanted to suffocate him. The poet waited until there were fewer people and then took his turn in going forward, dragging Michel by the arm. Michel, who was intimidated and embarrassed by his guide's exuberance, would have preferred to stay by himself. The musician appeared to have been plunged into a sort of ecstasy. A few tears were rolling down his cheeks. Was it his success, or the beauty of the work he had just interpreted? The poet introduced the student from the conservatory.

"Outside the conservatory, do you give lessons?" the musician asked.

Michel misunderstood and thought the pianist was offering to teach him. He replied that unfortunately he didn't have the means. The misunderstanding was soon cleared up. The poet thought it good to add, "He certainly needs to earn a little money. His father died during the war in tragic circumstances. I'll tell you about it."

These last words were accompanied by a host of gestures, a grimace, and a wink. Once more Michel felt humiliated, different. But by now the musician was looking for someone in the crowd.

"Muriel, where is Muriel?"

He ended up bringing to his side a tall brown-haired woman.

"My dear friend, did you not tell me you were looking for a piano teacher for your girl? I have found just what you need."

Michel didn't have time to say he was already giving lessons and running from neighborhood to distant neighborhood, from the Avenue des Gobelins to the Parc Monceau, from Passy to the Faubourg Saint-Martin. "There's even one in Vincennes, the bastard!" For consolation, he told himself, "At least I'll get to know Paris."

The woman, Muriel Lemoigne, agreed immediately.

One, two, three, Michel thought, amazed: the poet, the musical clown, the brunette, no one has heard me play a note, and they trust me! I didn't even have to ask for anything. I didn't utter a word!

On the Rue de Vaugirard near the Boulevard des Invalides, one crossed under an archway and entered a garden in the midst of which four little houses were lined up. Michel rang the bell of the last house. Muriel Lemoigne came to open the door for him. She called her daughter, Jacotte. But Michel was so surprised by the decor, he barely paid attention to the child. The woman realized it and started to laugh.

"I've never seen any place like it. But for me it's very amusing to live here. Would you like a tour?"

There were many little rooms, all of them leading to short staircases. The windows were decorated with panes of blue and orange glass. What remained of the original furniture was in the purest Art Deco style. Michel noticed a big dressing table made of stucco, covered in silver paint and equipped with a mirror whose smoked glass gave off golden reflections. There were chairs made of steel tubes. The Bauhaus had passed this way.

"Are you familiar with Freud?" said Muriel Lemoigne. "This villa is the work of a mad architect who suffered from a violent Oedipus complex. All these rooms with their stairways converge toward the central point, his mother's bedroom."

"Do you know what became of them?"

"The mother is dead, and he left."

"He could have made it into a mausoleum."

The young woman snickered.

"That's exactly what I tell myself. I have the impression of being locked inside a mausoleum."

"And who lives in the mother's room?"

"I do, of course."

It was decided that Michel would come twice a week to the strange house on the Rue de Vaugirard. Jacotte was a little girl of about ten, thin and quiet, very dark, always pensive. Thirty years later when he took care of Emma and gave her her first lessons, she suddenly reminded him of Jacotte, buried for so long in oblivion.

The comparison with the mausoleum soon gave way to another metaphor. For Michel that house was a spider's web. Little by little, one was drawn toward the center where she who must devour you was waiting. And soon enough he was devoured, to his great pleasure.

12

 "Do you know how I met Arderiu?" Florence asked.

"You were his student."

"Yes, but how I became his student."

At that time the musician had been living in a villa behind the Haute-Plante.* One spring day when he opened his window, he heard someone playing the piano in a nearby villa across the garden: Bach's Partitas. He listened. The playing wasn't bad. But in the third one, a wrong note made him grimace.

The next day at the same time, he again heard the Partitas. And in the third one, the wrong note. On the following days, it was the same. Finally he couldn't take it anymore. He went outside, following the sounds to find the house from which the music was coming. He asked to see the musician. When he found himself face-to-face with Florence, he said in his terrible accent, "Mademoiselle, every day you play the wrong note in the third Partita, and I can't stand it any longer."

Florence added, "He looked really angry. I was afraid."

Arderiu protested. "She pretended to be afraid."

As the Catalan maestro wished, the three musicians decided only to take students who had already reached a decent level.

"I am the only one," remarked Michel, "to whom you have taught everything. How to read the notes, how to place my fingers on the keys for the first time . . ."

* A town square in Pau. *Trans.*

"Well in fact, no, you're not the only one. I had one other little student before."

"In Barcelona, in Paris, in Alicante?"

"No. Here in Pau. Just about the same time as I was trying to bring the art of the piano into your head and your hands."

A woman, Aline Meunier, had come looking for him after one of his concerts. She told him she admired him and never missed one. She must have arrived in our city at about the same time he did. Previously she had always lived in the colonies. Her father was probably a governor or a bureaucrat of some sort. She showed him a photo from her childhood, taken in Laos. They were carrying her in a palanquin, and she was looking gravely into the camera. For now, she had come from Bingerville in the Ivory Coast. She was alone. Widowed or divorced, she didn't specify. She seemed to have a bit of money and didn't work.

Arderiu did not say what their relationship was, but knowing him . . . He limited himself to one detail: "She had nice legs."

He added, "She was a bit overexcited. She started sending me letters. She wrote that she had known great hardship. 'Life has taken everything from me. I still suffer from what others have done to me.'"

She asked him if he would consent to meet with her. She had something very important to ask him. She suggested meeting in a tea shop. This kind of place was part of her idea of elegance, of life in society. Arderiu accepted.

"I've still never seen you refuse a woman anything," Michel said.

So as he sat with his cup of tea and cream cakes, she told him she had had a child, an adorable little boy. He was called René. At the age of three, he had been killed in an accident, crushed by the trunk of a tree that was being cut down and fell outside its expected path. She said, "I wanted him to go to Naval Academy. I wondered how I was going to finance his studies. All I had to pay for was his little casket, all in white."

Arderiu was politely compassionate. Aline Meunier seemed to have forgotten him, to be speaking to herself: "I used to kiss my child with little pecks. He would laugh." She even began to sing a lullaby: "Sleep, sleep, my dear little angel, the sandman is here . . ."

"Up to that point, everything seemed very normal," said Arderiu. "She was crying a little. I took her hands in mine. She had a lovely silhouette; her clothes were very tastefully chosen. The tea was cold in her cup. She apologized, 'I'm wasting your time.' And it was then that she put her request into words: 'Would you be willing to teach my little boy to play the piano? For him to be your student? . . .'"

The musician took a moment to understand what she was talking about, what she was suggesting. "She wanted to pay me for these lessons!"

"So the little student you had at the same time as I . . ."

"Was dead."

Unbeknown to Michel, the son of Aline Meunier, this child whose body had long since been digested by the tropical soil, became his double. When Michel studied his pink book of piano exercises, Arderiu described to Aline Meunier the progress and the mistakes of his imaginary student. Strangely considerate, the teacher now reassured him. "Don't be jealous. I never told her that her son was as talented as you were."

Still they had progressed together, struggling over Hanon's *The Virtuoso Pianist,* then over the Czerny method.

"Was he admitted to the conservatory with me?"

A moot question, since Michel only went to the conservatory because Arderiu had run off with Florence. He corrected his question: "What stage was he at when you left Pau?"

The game had long since ended. Aline Meunier went bankrupt in the crash of 1929. She didn't know what to do, was incapable of finding work. When she was totally without resources, Arderiu, in whom she confided, offered her money, but she refused. "I'm going to leave," she said. "I'm going to return down there near my little boy."

He thought she had found a way to go back to the Ivory Coast. But he soon received a letter. She thanked him for the piano lessons. She announced that with the few francs she had left, she had gotten a train ticket to Biarritz. She wanted to see the ocean again. And the sea, well, it was strong there, and she was certainly a good swimmer, but the waves would carry her away. She said good-bye to him, adding, "I love you for everything, for your art, for your life, your tears, your joys, your pain, your hopes, your despair . . ."

Arderiu never heard from her again, and he never knew whether around that time they found a woman drowned in Biarritz.

13

Nicolau Arderiu was at his piano, pounding out a strange thing full of dissonances; he was hammering at it, abusing the sustain pedal. Michel asked him what he was playing.

"I'm composing the music for my burial, a funeral ode."

"It's certainly high time."

"Swear you'll play it at my funeral. Who knows, perhaps I will hear it in my sepulchral sleep."

"You'd do better to remember that June is approaching. Florence is going to be thirty. Any ideas?"

"We could give a concert . . ."

But there wasn't going to be a party for Florence's thirtieth birthday, and Nicolau Arderiu would never have a burial.

On June 12, 1944, at seven thirty in the morning, the musician, carrying a suitcase, his overcoat, an umbrella, surrounded by armed soldiers, climbed painfully into a German military truck set high on its wheels. Florence stood on the steps. As soon as the truck had disappeared, she ran to the telephone and called Michel: "Come right away. They've arrested Nicolau."

When Michel arrived, he found Florence in her bathrobe, gathering up papers, musical scores, laundry. No room in the villa had been spared the search.

"They arrived at seven in the morning. The *Feldwebel* who was in charge announced to Nicolau that he was arresting him as a hostage. 'Why me?' Nicolau asked. He replied, 'In this town, you are a well-known man, a bigwig. And in your past there is the Frente Popular. We are very well informed.' That is what he told him, word for word."

Michel wondered whom they could ask to intervene. But neither in Florence's family—from whom, besides, she had remained estranged—nor among their friends was there anyone who consorted with the occupiers. Of course, there were the Merlins, big business people who appeared to be collaborating. They were mostly frightened, ready to make any concession in order to prevent their son Charles, a spoiled brat, from being sent to the S.T.O.,* and were too cowardly to count on.

"Come in the kitchen; there's still some coffee."

They served themselves two cups of ersatz brew and sat on either side of the white wooden table.

"I packed his suitcase, and I asked if I could make him some coffee. The *Feldwebel* told me I had one half-hour. Nicolau dressed and drank his coffee. He picked the score of *The Art of the Fugue* up off the ground and added it to his suitcase, with no one, neither himself nor the Germans, making any comment. You know how nervous, emotional he is. And today from the beginning to the end, from the arrival of the soldiers to the moment when he got into the truck, he stayed totally calm."

"*The Art of the Fugue.* Do you think he took it on purpose?"

"I don't think so. It was the score he had started working on a few days earlier, Karl Czerny's arrangement for piano."

The Art of the Fugue is an unfinished work. Bach died composing it. Michel put no stock in omens, but still he was choked with anxiety.

Florence rose and rinsed the cups in the sink. She made her way toward the living room, and Michel followed her, his arms dangling.

"Can I help you clean up?"

"Later."

She collapsed into an armchair.

* Service du Travail Obligatoire (s.t.o.) was the obligatory work service in Germany. *Trans.*

"I told him to take a coat, and he wanted to take his hat and his umbrella as well."

"An umbrella to go to prison!"

"It's just like him. But wait, here's something even more like him. At the moment they took him away, he kissed me, then he said: 'I had a lesson this afternoon with Anne Bousquet at her house. Can you get in touch with her? I wouldn't want her to wait for me for nothing.'"

So, Michel thought, Anne Bousquet might be the last of Nicolau Arderiu's beautiful students. And Florence seemed to be thinking the same thing.

"We've always taken him as he is," Michel said. "The umbrella and the rest."

But suddenly Florence weakened. Her mauve-lidded eyes filled with tears. She came and held Michel. She smelled of the night, sweat, weeping.

Eight other hostages had been arrested in town. They were locked in the army barracks in a separate building that had formerly been an infirmary. They stayed there for five days. They could receive visitors and packages. Florence and Michel went to see Nicolau each day. They stayed together in the infirmary garden. Nicolau appeared serene. His friends and visitors began to speak of his courage.

The last visit, Friday the sixteenth, was extended until ten in the evening. After that was a curfew. Watching Florence and Michel depart, Arderiu hummed:

Adios muchachos
Compañeros de mi vida . . .

One of those tangos that he used to say makes your heart spin. Then his voice broke.

Michel accompanied Florence to the villa. He stayed there to sleep. In fact, there was a room he used anytime it was too late to go all the way back to the hillside. They had decided to get up at dawn to try to watch the depar-

ture of the prisoners. They saw two buses leaving the barracks. They learned later that one bus was full of hostages
and political prisoners, the other full of Jews who had just
been rounded up in the region, and that the buses wouldn't
go any further than Dax. The detainees were taken next
by train to Bordeaux. One man died during this brief trip.
They were imprisoned at Fort Haa, guarded by the SS. Then
they were part of a convoy to Dachau. Once again, Nicolau
Arderiu, snatched away, was disappearing. Alas, it wasn't a
woman taking him, but death in one of its most hideous
incarnations. Less than a year later, with the war over, the
camps discovered in all their horror, it was clear he would
not return.

14

 For a long time, if not forever, the Catalan maestro haunted Michel, who, sometimes consciously, sometimes unconsciously, never stopped following his example, all the while persuaded he could never be anything but a poor imitation.

One of the first consequences of this state of mind was that he thought he was in love with Florence. They had continued running the music school together. Before Nicolau Arderiu's arrest, the young woman had already been acting as a musical assistant. More and more often, Michel stayed at the villa in the evening. The absent man was between them.

One morning in the kitchen as she was making coffee, Florence told him: "I had a strange dream. We were both getting on a bus, an old yellow bus that was supposed to take us to Toulouse. Inside it was packed. We found seats all the way in back on a bench that made a half circle. I was waiting for the driver to get on board down at the other end, far away, because at the same time the bus had become an immense concert hall, perhaps a church. I told myself that during the whole trip, I could snuggle up against you, sleep . . ."

"Maybe the dream comes from the bus that took Nicolau away."

The war ended, and they learned of Arderiu's death. Little by little, the tension between them grew. Each time Michel desired Florence, he resolved hypocritically not to make the first move. But he already considered inevitable what was going to happen.

Florence was seated at the piano, absentmindedly playing one of Satie's *Gymnopédies*. Michel came up and stood behind her. And suddenly he grabbed her forearms to correct their position.

"Like he did," she said.

That day she had put her hair up. She added, "Do you like the back of my neck? It's my neck that seduced him."

Michel leaned forward and gave her a kiss in the hollow of her shoulder. She continued playing the slow and resigned song, which was nothing like her. He let go of her arms and put his hands on her breasts.

He stepped back.

That night she said, "Stay with me."

He remembered Nicolau Arderiu's brief confession: " 'Take me away!' That's what she told me."

Michel Mailhoc moved in with Florence. He only went up to La Paix to see his mother.

As the disciple and former colleague of the deported musician, he was wooed by several political movements and parties. The communists, the socialists, the Gaullists pressured him for support. He refused, or rather he avoided them, slipping between their fingers. In his heart, he thought it all had nothing to do with him, that he was outside the game.

Around the same time, the city decided to pay solemn homage to Nicolau Arderiu. The first idea was to play Mozart's Requiem in one of the two major churches of the city, Saint-Martin or Saint-Jacques. But it was too ambitious a plan. There was no longer an orchestra, apart from a few amateur groups. Finally an evening concert was planned at the municipal Saint-Louis Theater located inside the city hall. Florence, Michel, and some other students of the pianist played his favorite pieces: Mozart, Schubert, Schumann, Brahms, Albeniz, Ravel. This memorial was not unanimously endorsed. Michel and Florence's affair was beginning to be known, and it scandalized people. It had already cost them students. The last piece of the evening, played by Michel, was the one Arderiu had composed in preparation for his burial. Full of dissonances, it disturbed the audience. They thought that the deceased, who had been for a time one of the city's most spectacular characters, was clearly a strange person. Not to mention his friends. Of course, the Nazis had made a martyr of him. But after all, a foreigner . . .

Several months later, Michel and Florence again crossed the threshold of the city hall. This time it was not for a concert in the municipal theater. Accompanied by two witnesses, they went discreetly to the marriage chambers. Geneviève Mailhoc did not take part in the ceremony. While it is true that mothers tend to love their sons a little too much, Florence was doubly a rival.

2 The Hygrometer

I

He had just finished playing "Tea for Two," "The Man I Love," then "Adios Muchachos" (a pathetic homage to Nicolau Arderiu), "La Habanera" from *Carmen* and an arrangement of the *Concierto de Aranjuez,* then "Swanee" and "Just a Gigolo." Softly he started in on Chopin's Etude no. 3, op. 10 in E Major. The only "serious" piece allowed, which the proximity of Valdemosa even made obligatory. The customers understood the allusion and appreciated it. Poor Chopin, ending up there with his shrewish wife and his ailing lungs. The piano, a Pleyel that he had so much trouble getting delivered, must still be rotting between the humid walls of the charterhouse.

Suddenly Michel was ashamed of dishing out Chopin to the few idle rich, who seemed to be bored in this luxury hotel. (The Balearics weren't yet invaded by masses of tourists, charters from Germany.) There was a smattering of applause, lost in the noise of conversation and clinking glasses, which put the finishing touches on his distress. Chopin wanted to be classical, like Mozart. He thought that mastering the fugue meant understanding the logic that guided all music. And here was Michel, trotting him out in a piano bar.

Just as he did everyday, he gave a little thought to that musician on the Rue de Rome, the policeman's lover, whose fingers flying on the keyboard made him understand Chopin. And a thought to James Warner, with whom he had first played jazz, painfully aping Fats Waller and Duke Ellington. He closed his keyboard and rose. As he passed by their table, three or four customers applauded him again. He crossed the large hallway, which looked out onto the garden on one side and onto the beach on the other. He went out the beach side. He slung his white jacket over his arm, pulled off his bow tie, returned to the bungalow. Marie-Christine wasn't there. She must have gone swimming.

He started preparing dinner. He found some eggs in the fridge and boiled them. He cut some tomatoes for a salad, added black olives. With the leftover cheese and some fruit, that would be enough. They could have taken their meals at the hotel, but in the kitchen along with the staff, and he couldn't inflict such a thing on Marie-Christine.

He was just putting the plates on the table when she arrived, blond and golden. She apologized, but he told her he was glad; he had accepted this job so she could enjoy the sun and the sea.

"I'm hungry," she said, rubbing her flat stomach.

After dinner they took a walk among the pines. The sun was setting behind some small islands.

"We should go out there one day," said Marie-Christine.

"I don't know if you can rent boats."

"Of course you can."

"It's got to be too expensive."

"Forgive me. I hadn't thought about that. I always forget we're poor."

"More precisely, that you're living with a man who is poor."

It was time to go back and take up his duties behind the piano.

Every evening at this precise hour, Michel felt guilty. Leaving Marie-Christine alone during the day, that was one thing. But at night. She said, "I read, I watch TV. Don't worry."

Often he found her asleep, nude on the bed like a gift from heaven.

On the beach they had noticed a fellow who greatly

amused them. He was a guest at the hotel, an Italian, the perfect prototype of the Latin lover. He had a patented technique. As soon as he met a woman, he invited her to take a ride with him on a pedal boat on the bay. This tactic furnished them with endless jokes. Inexpensive, the pedal boat. But to make love in such a contraption you had to be an acrobat.

It was doubtless this comic character who prompted them to rent a pedal boat themselves one afternoon for a brief ride. The hotel had a little flotilla for use by its guests.

They left the beach. The bay was almost enclosed, so the water was as calm as a lake's. They didn't follow the shore-line but cut straight across. Steering by gently pedaling was actually very amusing. They wondered again how the Italian lover managed when he tried to push his luck all the way. Michel indulged in a parody that almost made both of them fall out of the boat. Then they started to steer properly again.

The great expanse of water was deserted, as if it had been reserved for them. In the distance for two or three days, one could make out a very large yacht that had dropped anchor at the mouth of the bay. Curiosity led them to approach it. It was one of the most beautiful pleasure boats imaginable.

"What if we took a tour?" said Marie-Christine.

Approaching closer, still pedaling on their ridiculous little craft, they came alongside the hull of the port side? Starboard side? It must be starboard, Michel decided.

"In a film," he said, "or in a bestseller, there would be someone on deck who would see us, yell 'Hallo!' and invite us on board."

Scarcely had he pronounced these words when they heard someone yelling above them.

"Marie-Christine! Qu'est-ce que tu fais là! What are you doing there?"

A young man dressed in white pants and a shirt of an un-definable color but of exquisite tone leaned over the railing.

"We're taking a tour!" yelled Marie-Christine with a touch of insolence.

"Come on up!"

The young man disappeared, doubtless to go give a few orders. Sailors busied themselves. A ladder, or rather a veritable staircase, was lowered along the side of the yacht. A sailor came down with a rope and attached the pedal boat to the last rung of the banister. Without waiting for the sailor to reach out his hand to help her, Marie-Christine jumped on the ladder and swiftly climbed it.

Now they were on deck. Marie-Christine and the young man in the white pants kissed each other like old friends. Though he was coming from the sea, so to speak, Michel was embarrassed to be in his swimming trunks.

"So," said Marie-Christine by way of introductions. "This is Michel. Is this your boat?"

"No. It's my brother-in-law's."

"Is Mary here?"

"Of course."

Marie-Christine explained to Michel that David, the man in the white pants, had a sister who was married to a British manufacturer, someone in chemical engineering. Another sister, Glenda, had become a well-known movie actress.

"And Glenda?"

"She couldn't come. She's shooting a film in Kenya, with elephants, lions, pygmies, the whole bit."

Following David, they reached the back deck where a few people were getting some fresh air under an awning fluttering in the breeze. They were all dressed, and Michel felt as if he were in one of those nightmares where one finds oneself naked in the middle of a crowd. Marie-Christine, sure of herself and of her beauty, remained at ease in her two-piece bathing suit. After a moment she simply said she was a bit chilly, borrowed a shawl, and wrapped it around her shoulders. The bartender came to offer them a drink.

Michel knew he was the butt of jokes and not only because of what he was wearing. Questions weren't long in coming, which was really only natural, given their preposterous appearance.

"Did you know we were here?"

"Not in the least," said Marie-Christine.

"We were only getting a little exercise with that contraption," added Michel.

He gestured below to the lower regions where the pedal boat must be attached.

"Allora, lui è il tuo professore."

Why did they have to speak all these languages! Michel understood they were curious to finally see the music teacher for whom Marie-Christine had left everything. He heard or thought he heard: "Un po' troppo vecchio."

"Are you staying at the hotel? Apparently it's very nice."

"Better yet," said Marie-Christine. "We're in a little bungalow among the pines."

Suddenly they seemed to lose interest in him except to refill his glass. Marie-Christine spoke with this one and that one, obviously happy to have found her old friends. Michel began to experience the feeling of exclusion he knew only too well. As soon as a group seemed linked by habit, complicity, or as soon as someone spoke in front of him of something he didn't know about—whether it was a culinary specialty or a film—he became a stranger, a pariah, like one of his Cagot ancestors. At the same time, his natural benevolence made him more inclined to rejoice at seeing Marie-Christine reunited for a moment with her old friends and with the luxury she had given up because of him. Together they had come face-to-face with hard times, without a cent. How had she tolerated it? Such a proof of love, since there was no other explanation, filled him with a feeling of indignity and a desperate adoration. He didn't deserve such a girl. But if he lost her, it would kill him.

The young woman and these unknown people who seemed to be so close to her continued mixing French,

English, German, Italian. He didn't understand every-thing. He guessed they were asking her whether the two of them had ever gotten married. He was ashamed Marie-Christine was going to have to admit he hadn't managed to get a divorce, he couldn't seem to pull it off. But she gave a charming shrug of her shoulders and quipped, "Who wants to get married these days?"

A little later, Michel shuddered when he heard her tell a buxom blond in a black linen dress: "If you come ashore, you must pay us a visit. Just ask for the musician's bunga-low."

"You are so well known!" said the fat blond. "Do you give concerts? Excuse my ignorance."

"It doesn't matter," said Michel.

Once again they lost interest in him. He realized he was humming Etude in E Major to himself. He didn't believe in eternal life. The only interest he had in the possibility of life after death was that Chopin, Mozart, Schubert, Schu-mann, and a few others might be able to see from up on high how much he loved them, with an unsullied affection, the kind one never grants to the living, and the suffering of their lives, the indifference, the tears, would be erased.

On the horizon the sun was starting to set. A man dressed as a naval officer, probably the captain, came to find David and asked to speak with him.

"Excuse me," David said to Michel. "We get underway tomorrow morning. But we don't know yet whether we'll go towards Tangiers or towards the Costa Smeralda. I have to consult with the captain. But you must spend the evening with us."

"Only I can't," Michel said. "It's high time for me to go back."

"What, you can't?"

"No, I can't. But Marie-Christine, if she wants to . . ."

The words suddenly gathered in a bubble in his throat.

The young woman looked at him, and he read surprise but also joy in her eyes.

"Really, I could . . ." she murmured.

"Why not? You seem so happy to have found your friends."

"Marie-Christine can stay?" said David.

"And besides, I'm no longer very warm," Michel said.

"I could have lent you a shirt and a pair of pants."

"Thank you, but I need to go back."

"I'm coming with you," said Marie-Christine.

But he insisted she stay. Now his determination was becoming a bit masochistic. He went up to her and whispered in an aside, "For once you can have some fun. You know full well how sad your evenings are because of me . . ."

He bid farewell to the group with a wave, and each of them made a little sign. Marie-Christine had taken two steps back, as if she wanted some room to help with his departure. He waited for her to come give him a kiss, but she too was content to raise her hand in a timid little gesture. All that was left for him to do was to turn his back on all those people and even on Marie-Christine, to reach the ladder. But David stopped him.

"You're not going ashore on that contraption?"

He gave orders. They watched as a complex maneuver took place. A motorized dinghy, which Michel had not yet noticed because it was moored to the poop deck on the other side, starboard . . . no, port side, came to tow the pedal boat. Michel was invited to sit in the dinghy, which was driven by a man wearing a naval officer's cap. The dinghy took off. Michel thought it was going too fast and constantly turned around to keep an eye on the pedal boat, swaying in the wake. He told himself it could turn over at any moment. Every time he turned around he saw the yacht farther and farther away, shrinking, a child's toy, a model. He could no longer make out the passengers. The pedal boat was jumping about horribly. The fear of seeing it capsize kept him from thinking about anything else: that he would be late for the piano bar, that Marie-Christine had little difficulty letting him leave by himself while she stayed on board . . . on board the very marvelous yacht that was getting underway at dawn.

2

Robert Schumann, op. 126, Seven Pieces in Fughetta Form . . . This title awakened Michel's sense of irony about himself.* He wasn't lacking lucidity, even when his behavior resembled the oblique path of a bishop on a chess board. He was tempted to consider his gig at the Majorca piano bar demeaning, but he quickly invented an excuse: the great Maurice Ravel had been a pianist in the Granville Casino in Normandy. Only he wasn't Maurice Ravel. He blamed his pointless escapade on the imprint of Nicolau Arderiu's strong personality. If he had run off with a student and before, if he had let himself be seduced by Florence, his mentor's own wife, these were imitations. Or rather since he was a musician, variations on the theme his elder had shown him.

Marie-Christine was the daughter of a very rich man in the gas and oil business who had spent some time living in the Béarn because of the natural gas at Lacq. After her brief adventure with Michel, she returned to her milieu. As for Florence, after having refused a divorce when Michel wanted one, she began divorce proceedings against him just when he felt more or less inclined in his heart of hearts to return to their life together. She didn't wait long to remarry. She was one of those women who always finds a man, while others seem condemned to remain alone forever.

Geneviève had died sometime earlier from cancer when she was barely sixty-five. Her light-hearted soul had been reunited in musician's paradise with the man who had been executed and doubtless also with the other men she had

---

* *Fugue* in French also means "flight." *Trans.*

loved and with the charming Cléo. Michel moved to La
Paix. He told himself he had narrowly escaped coming
home to live with his mother. Without really knowing why,
he had decided against returning to Paris and trying to make
it there as a soloist. If you want to be an artist, you can't be
modest, Arderiu used to tell him. But Michel never knew
what to think of himself. Sometimes he thought giving up
Paris was precisely that, the true betrayal of his mentor. He
took up his work as a piano teacher and limited himself to
taking part in the occasional concert. With the other musicians of the city, he played sonatas for piano and viola and
put together a trio. His brother Denis had agreed to let him
have use of the family property. When he had come home
from his prison camp, the Pont et Chaussées engineer had
been posted to Antibes. He greatly enjoyed the Côte d'Azur
and had turned his back definitively on the Béarn.

Still, one summer Denis and his family came to spend
a few days of their vacation at La Paix. That's all it took
for Pascale to meet a young man at the tennis courts in
Beaumont Park, a man who sold sporting goods, André
Dufresne. A year later they were married. The wedding took
place in Antibes. Michel, once again the bachelor uncle,
traveled to it. He felt his fortieth birthday approaching, and
he had the leisure, through the rituals of this somewhat
stupid, somewhat false day, to be amazed at what a mess he
had made of his life and to wonder where he was heading.

After the wedding feast, they danced to the sound of a
little orchestra. The bride got it into her head to ask her
uncle to play something. He didn't want to. Led on by Pascale and her family, the entire wedding party soon began to
chant, "Michel to the piano! Michel to the piano!" He had
to perform.

He wondered what they expected of him. Probably some
pompous piece full of trills and trickles. But almost invol-
untarily—he had had a little to drink—there surged forth
from his fingers "Strangers in the Night" and the other

American standards he used to trot out at the hotel bar in the Balearics during his escapade with Marie-Christine. One of the musicians returned to his drum set and began to accompany him discreetly. The wedding party started to dance again.

Michel Mailhoc conjured up a fantasy. He was afraid the young married couple was going to want to move into the house in the Vallée Heureuse and he would have to move out. But it didn't interest them. Too far away, too inconvenient. They took a big apartment in town. Pascale set to having children: a girl, a boy, and another girl.

In August 1956 came the death of Yves Nat. At age sixteen, Michel had heard him in a recital, playing on an Erard at the Winter Palace in Pau, and from that day on, his admiration for Nat had been boundless. A century before Yves Nat, on July 29, 1856, Robert Schumann had been released from life. Michel wanted to mark this anniversary with an homage similar to the one Nicolau Arderiu had once given Schubert. But he had neither a vocalist nor an orchestra at hand. He gave an evening concert in October with *Scenes from Childhood,* the *Kreisleriana,* and the Sonata for Piano no. 1 in F-sharp Minor. It wasn't much of a success.

3

The trio to which Michel Mailhoc belonged—piano, violin, and cello—was invited to give a concert at the home of a German financier. Ugo Becker's business was in Munich. But he didn't lack for extra homes. He owned a castle in Bavaria, a property in Tuscany, and he had recently purchased a marble palace built along the hillside of the Jurançon by some English lord enamored of fox hunting. With a few minor changes, the heavy Elizabethan and Chippendale furniture had stayed put, giving the public rooms a severe and depressing aspect. Michel found himself in front of a superb Steinway, which he had a little trouble getting used to. The program he had chosen with his friends consisted of Beethoven's Trio, op. 97, *Archduke,* and Schubert's Trio in E-flat Major, which prompted the cellist, a phlegmatic bald fellow with glasses and a deadpan sense of humor, to quip, "You can't say we're taking many risks."

During the reception following the concert, Michel felt as though he were back on the yacht with Marie-Christine's friends and just as ill at ease. The musicians had to wear tails. Having to disguise himself in such an awkward manner was the only thing Michel didn't like about music.

Late in the evening, Ugo Becker took him aside.

"An idea came to me as I was listening to you. Perhaps you know I married a singer. Pauline was beginning her career when we met, and for me she gave up her calling."

"Did you insist upon it?" Michel asked boldly.

"Yes. And unfortunately she has suffered. She has become rather neurasthenic. Did you see how she behaves? She barely speaks to our guests: 'Hello! Thank you!' I won-

der if it wouldn't do her good to take up singing again—
as an amateur, of course. Would you agree to work with her
during our time here?"

"I am not a vocal coach. I could simply serve as her accompanist."

Ugo Becker brushed aside this concern with a wave of
his hand, meaning there was no reason to dwell on such a
detail. Michel asked if he could think about it.

"You know," said Ugo Becker point-blank, "if it's something that worries you, I was never a Nazi. I was twenty
years old in 1942, and I was sent to the Russian front as a
common soldier."

"And Madame Becker, what does she think of your plan?"

"I haven't spoken to her about it yet. The idea only came
to me just now. Give me your answer first."

After this conversation, Michel looked around the audience for this woman he had only glimpsed upon his arrival.
He didn't find her. She must have left the party, disdaining
her duties as hostess.

Two days later he took his car—a recent acquisition—
and went to the marble palace. If he'd been asked what
struck him most when he found himself face-to-face with
Pauline Becker, he would have replied: "She was wearing
blue jeans and gold sandals." A perfectly vulgar outfit, but
which on her, wasn't.

The evening of the concert, he had the impression that
she was tall, and now he saw it wasn't at all true. Still, she
seemed imposing. The impression came from her face with
its very structured architecture, her large forehead, high
cheekbones, her large but well-shaped nose, her opulent
blond hair. She must have been around forty. She spoke
with the affected intonation of high society. When he was
surprised she didn't have the slightest German accent, she
told him she was from Lausanne.

"Can't you tell?"

There was also her perfume, a mix of grass and pepper.

She wanted to begin working right away. She led him to the huge space she called the music room, where the trio had given its concert. The name amused Michel because his mother had also called the little hole where she closed herself off to practice her viola a music room. It was a joke. How often had he heard her through the door, playing her favorite piece, Vieuxtemps's *Capriccio?* Later at the rare times when he happened to hear this seldom-played work on the radio or in concert, his eyes filled with tears.

Pauline Becker had prepared a score of lieder by Sergei Rachmaninoff, which she sang in Russian. Her voice lacked volume, but Michel found she had a good technique and especially sensitivity. As for the woman, she was close to seducing him. So aristocratic—he didn't like the word, but he couldn't find another one—and at the same time simple and modest.

4

 Before the concert at the Beckers, Michel had felt the need for a haircut. He disliked the boy he usually went to, Jean. But he didn't have the nerve to change. Jean sounded like a pimp making him an offer:

"We have a manicurist now. Doesn't that appeal to you?"

His whole life, Michel had never trusted his extremities to a manicurist. He said no, then he thought twice. It would be better to go play the piano at these people's house with elegant hands.

"My name is Monique," said the manicurist as she seated herself on a little stool next to him, while Jean continued to work on his hair.

She took his right hand and was surprised: "What short nails you have! Almost none!"

"Monsieur Mailhoc is a pianist," Jean piped in.

"Me too. I took piano before," Monique said. "And then, you know how it is, I couldn't continue. But they said I was talented."

"You're not going to start in on your life story," said Jean nastily.

"Why shouldn't she?" Michel retorted.

"Now I have a son. He's ten. I send him to music school, but he doesn't want to do anything. Just like at grade school. He doesn't work. I'm raising him on my own, so he gets away with a lot."

The manicurist was wearing a blouse that buttoned in the front. When she shifted position, she crossed her legs. She had a beauty mark just above her knee on her right inner thigh.

She said her husband had been a sergeant, a paratrooper on the military base at Pau who was killed in Algeria. Michel couldn't help thinking that those paratroopers, wandering about off duty with their camouflage fatigues, their boots, their shaved heads under red berets, were ruining the streets of the city for him. Not to mention the souvenir shops that sold little "paras" and all sorts of trinkets connected with them. In his youth they hadn't been there and in fact didn't even exist. Even though he knew it wasn't reasonable, he hated everything that clouded his images of the past.

When Michel handed a tip to the manicurist as he left, she refused it. She asked him if he wouldn't be willing to give piano lessons to her son. Perhaps he could succeed in doing something with him: at the music school there was no supervision; they weren't strict enough. He responded that he only took on students who were already at an advanced level. She looked undone. He ended up saying yes, perhaps because he was distracted; he was thinking of her beauty mark.

5

 In the music room there was a large portrait of Pauline, but it was unfinished. She was pictured standing, glowing in blondness, her outline lengthened by a red dress with a train.

"Bernadette Lanner is in the midst of finishing this painting. She works on it every time I'm in the region. She's a friend, my best friend. Today she's practically given up painting. What a pity!"

"She's given up painting; you've given up singing. Everyone has given up, if I understand right."

"My husband bought me. He bought you too, in a way. He's entrusting me to you to get some peace and quiet."

Ugo Becker had to go back to Munich. He announced to Michel, "My wife is going to stay a while in the Béarn. I hope you are going to continue working with her. It does her a world of good."

Michel responded that he was a pianist, not a doctor. He asked how long Pauline Becker was planning to stay.

"I have no idea. She is free."

When Michel left the interview, Pauline, who had been waiting for him, asked, "Did he tell you I was crazy? That's what he likes to tell people, usually."

Michel protested and assured her the word had not been uttered, but that was certainly what Ugo Becker had meant to say.

6

Christophe, the son of the manicurist and the paratrooper, was big and strong for his age. From the looks of it, the need for physical activity was greater in him than the taste for school-work or the art of music. When he sat down at the piano, he looked like a calf. Or else he showed absolutely no interest and fell asleep, keeping his wits in reserve for other purposes.

"I don't know how to handle him," Monique Gérard had said when she brought him for the first time. "When Fabrice was killed, I thought I could count on my brother-in-law. He promised me he'd take care of him, be a substitute father. I soon understood he wanted to replace him in another way. I put him in his place. From that day on, he showed no more interest in us. As if this child, his brother's own son, didn't exist. We don't see him anymore."

Monique spoke next about the grandparents. On her husband's side, they hated her, as if she were responsible for the death of their son. On her side, her father was dead and her mother had remarried a good but weak man. Besides, they had gone off to live in the Languedoc near Nîmes.

Michel saw that Monique Gérard was never stingy in confiding about her catastrophic past.

It was soon clear that Christophe had no aptitude for the piano and that even if he had, he wouldn't have wanted to take advantage of it. As soon as he got to know his teacher a little, he found excuses to skip his lessons, and sometimes he didn't even bother to find excuses. Michel informed Monique. There was no sense continuing. The young woman was undone.

"And yet with a master teacher like you, I imagined . . ."
She didn't know whether to thank him or to apologize.
"You should steer him toward sports. Track, rugby."
"I don't know; he's so undisciplined!"
Michel offered to help her. She took on a defeated look
and told him he didn't need to bother with such a worry.
It was her problem, hers alone. Her problem and her cross
to bear.

7

"I don't like your house very much, but the grounds are splendid. I have a passion for grounds."

Michel was pleased he had allowed himself to criticize something belonging to Pauline Becker, as if it were a sign they were becoming more intimate.

"And you, in the Vallée Heureuse, do you have grounds?"

"You've got to be kidding! We both live on hillsides, but you can't compare. I have a simple garden, and, in any case, I am incapable of taking care of it. Someone looks after it. But you must come see it."

They took a brief stroll down paths that curved majestically, admiring cedars, magnolias, paulownias along the way. They walked to the former stables, demoted to the status of garage.

"I tell myself sometimes I ought to have horses. Before I used to ride a lot."

Clearly one could believe the life she had accepted to lead alongside Ugo Becker was composed of renunciations. Or else that renunciation was an attitude she was comfortable with. The remainder of their conversation supplied a new example.

"A role I would have liked is the Marschallin in *Der Rosenkavalier*. A character who renounces with so much grace . . ."

"Again!"

Pauline Becker began to sing softly:

I'm in the mood
when I'm so conscious of the frailty of everything
earthly.

deep down in my heart,
how we can hold nothing,
how we can hug nothing,
how everything slips through our fingers,
everything we grasp for dissolves,
everything fades like mist or a dream.

Michel never knew how much of Pauline's attitude was sincerity and how much was provocation.

"Still, this mustn't prevent many men from falling in love with you."

"Do you think? I always have the impression of being the one no one notices, the one left in her corner."

Going back to the house, she took his arm.

They passed by a gardener, who was in the process of transplanting some seedlings, for it was the beginning of spring. Pauline spoke a few kind words to him. Then continuing on their path and still leaning on Michel, she said, "He is like the gardener in *Elective Affinities*. Faced with the infinite field of botany, he is horror struck. If I didn't force him, there would be nothing but roses."

"I'll have to read *Elective Affinities*."

"*Die Wahlverwandtschaften*. Forgive me, I'm a bit Germanic."

Michel thought that this might be one of those books that can serve as a link, a messenger, a code between a man and a woman who don't yet dare admit to their feelings.

"Edouard and Ottilie, Charlotte and the Captain," his companion was saying, dreaming out loud.

Back at the house, she started looking on a bookshelf.

"Since we're speaking about books and since we both live on this hillside, I must tell you that someone lent me Nabokov's memoir, *Conclusive Evidence,* because he talks about his uncle who used to live here, just like we do now. On an estate you certainly know, Perpigna!"

Suddenly Geneviève's memories came back to him: the

concerts at Perpigna, the estate of the Russian prince with the impossible name, whom everyone called Rouka for short. He also thought of the time when bike trips with his friend James Warner were his principal distraction. One evening they came upon a kind of little palace, and that was Perpigna.

Ugo Becker returned briefly to Pau. He appeared satisfied that Michel Mailhoc was continuing to work with Pauline.

"She's talented," said Michel. "She truly loves music. It's even deeper. It's as if she's found a country where she is comfortable, at home."

"And she found this country again, thanks to you."

These words were uttered in such an ambiguous tone that Michel feared he would have to deal with an outburst of jealousy. He was already telling himself that he didn't know how to avoid a scene. Ugo Becker was leaving silences between his sentences.

"They say you are very appealing to your students."

He had surely heard about the episode with Marie-Christine.

"My dear man, I have nothing to fear from you. My wife always seeks to seduce, to arouse. But she loves no one. Her goodness, her sweetness, her sorrow can create illusions. She is cold and indifferent."

When he came home from the marble palace, Michel found a letter. On the envelope and at the top of the letterhead was a drawing of the château of the good King Henri. Colored paper for tourists. Monique Gérard was writing him to apologize once again and to thank him for the patience he had shown with Christophe.

"It is not about him that I would like to speak with you now but about me, if you'll permit it. I am alone and suffocating in a mediocre environment. Yet I love books, music. They have always been a passion for me. But I have no one to guide me, to tell me what is beautiful, what is good. I need someone to spend a few minutes with me from time to time, to speak with me, to tell me what records I must buy. Someone like you. If my request irritates you, don't answer. But now that I have had the chance to know you, I would feel more than ever excluded from the world you have given me a glimpse of."

Monique Gérard signed off "with my respect."

In his mailbox, there was also a score he had ordered from Paris: Carl Maria von Weber's *Die Temperamente beim Verluste der Geliebten,* known in French as *Quatre tempéraments amoureux:* "Four Romantic Temperaments."

8

 Whenever he got to Pauline Becker's and after they had settled in the music room, she always said, "Tell me what's new."

In general he replied, "There's not much to tell. I'm a bit of a woodsman."

"I, on the contrary, have so much to tell, I don't know where to start."

But they were society stories. Michel would scowl. He felt like a foreigner, with Pauline suddenly revolving on a planet located at the other end of the galaxy.

He offered her the score of Weber's lieder and proposed they work on it.

"It seems that these four lieder are like a portrait gallery of four rejected lovers. But you're the one who knows German."

Pauline Becker read the poems. Without translating them, she summarized for the pianist: "One of them manages with irony, the other expresses his despair, the other his anger . . ."

"And the last one?"

"Indifference."

They began to sight-read the score and worked for more than an hour. As Michel was leaving, Pauline thanked him. "You are so nice! I want to kiss you."

They exchanged two kisses on the cheek. Michel attempted to drift toward her lips. Pauline stepped back and said kindly but firmly, "No."

"I'm the fifth rejected lover?" said Michel.

"You are not a lover, and you are not rejected."

From then on, to say hello and goodbye they exchanged kisses. But Pauline continued withholding her lips.

Later she got in the habit of calling him almost every day. She gave him presents: a cigarette lighter, a scarf, liquor. Even on those occasions, if he tried to take her in his arms, she pushed him away. What good were those presents anyway, since what he wanted was their giver.

9

 "So you accept!"

Michel Mailhoc had arranged to meet Monique Gérard in a café on the Boulevard des Pyrénées. The sun was shining so brightly that winter day that they sat out on the terrace.

"I brought you two records," he said. "Schubert's Quintet for Strings and Mozart's Piano Concerto No. 17."

Monique protested. She had asked him to recommend records, not to give them to her.

"It's my pleasure for starters," said Michel. "What would you like to drink?"

"No alcohol. I can't tolerate it."

She ordered fruit juice. Once she was over her initial shyness, she started to talk, almost without ever changing her tone, as if she weren't in the midst of participating in an improvised conversation but rather reciting a speech that could have gone on endlessly once the gears were set in motion. Her difficult child, Christophe, her husband, her family, her in-laws, her work, her colleague Jean, all of them paraded before him in a tally of her woes.

"After they brought my husband's body back from Algeria, he was buried in his village near Vicq in the Gers. When I arrived, his parents wouldn't speak to me. I had brought Christophe, who was only five. My own parents couldn't come. That's what they said, but what I think is they didn't want to. They stayed in the Gard. I said to Christophe, 'Go kiss Grandpa and Grandma.' But he was afraid and clung to me. I insisted. He said, 'I want to see the rabbits.' On the rare occasions when we had come to the farm, he had been crazy about the rabbits. The old man yelled, 'See how she's raising him!' They placed the coffin on a trestle in the courtyard. They had covered it with a flag and on that had placed a cushion with his decorations and his red beret. There were a few locals, not many because the old man had feuded with everyone. We waited. No one dared speak. The courtyard wasn't even clean. We were practically wading in manure, and I was afraid to stain my black stockings. My shoes were already filthy. Chickens were running between our legs. They could have caged the chickens at least! There were also geese, who squawked because we were disturbing their routine. I have to admit his confit d'oie and foie gras are excellent. It's the region for it. Finally the detachment arrived for the military salute. We left for the church and cemetery. The ceremony was perfect. The coffin carried by the soldiers, the bugles playing taps . . . Except that his parents did not shed a single tear. Afterward we came back to the farm. I saw they had prepared a meal for the wake. My mother-in-law took off her veil and her hat and put on an apron. I asked her, 'Would you like me to help you?' Then the old man said, 'You are not invited. Our son didn't ask our advice before he married you. It was so he could be with whores like you that he enlisted in the army and died.' His other son, the one who afterward proved so eager to take care of me, tried to say a word or two, but the old man shut him up. I said, 'What is your problem? I've never done you any harm.' He said, 'Yes you have, you are a bad woman. God made you bad.' He got up and spoke again. 'The little one, you're going to leave him here.' He approached Christophe. He saw the child was holding a doll in his hand, a little paratrooper. I had let him bring it along so he'd be quiet. The old man grabbed the paratrooper from him, threw it on the floor, and smashed it with his heel against the kitchen tile. He jumped up and down in a grotesque manner, as if the floor were burning him. Christophe started to scream. I took him in my arms, and I left without saying a word. When he heard the sound of the engine, the old man came outside and yelled, 'And the car, is it yours or my son's?' I shot back, 'Mine! In my name!' He insisted, 'In your name but paid for with my son's money!' I started the car. I would have liked to run him over. I told Christophe I would buy him another toy, but he didn't want me to, as though there were only one in the world, irreplaceable, the one the old man had trampled . . . I'm boring you with my stories. Forgive me."

10

Pauline Becker had to return to Munich. She couldn't say when she might return. Probably in three months, but it wasn't up to her.

"Yet your husband told me one day that you were free."

"He claims I am. But it isn't always true."

The singing lesson was over. They had left the music room and were having a drink, sitting next to each other on the couch. Pauline started confiding. "I've been married for ten years, and my husband has never loved me. He found me decorative for a while. Now I bore him."

"Does he have someone else in his life?"

"No. He's not interested in women. What counts is business, power. He is always very polite, very courteous with me, attentive. But he'll never take me in his arms, never give me a caress. Even a dog needs to be petted."

"Especially a dog."

Michel laid a hand on her shoulder. She took his arm and pushed it away. The musician no longer knew what to think.

Ugo Becker had told him that his wife didn't love anyone, that she was cold. And now Pauline was complaining about her husband for the same reason.

"I don't understand your life at all."

"My life is rather sad."

A melodramatic line, but said so naturally it seemed completely sincere with no histrionics.

"And I, what am I to you?"

"I like you more and more. I can no longer imagine being deprived of our music lessons and our conversations."

("Tell me what's new." "There's not much to tell." "I, on

the contrary, have so much to tell . . ." Michel thought to himself with irony.)

He asked her if she would be glad to see her castle again. A castle in Bavaria! She groaned. "A castle! I ought to call it a prison!"

Nothing like the follies built by Ludwig of Bavaria. Ugo Becker had bought a sort of medieval fortress, perfectly sinister. When he shut himself away there with Pauline, it was a nightmare. She had the feeling she would never leave, that behind its thick walls she would have to submit to the bullying, to her husband's insults, or worse, to his silence, thick with disdain.

"You only know one aspect of my life. When I am at the castle, I remember, as if I could have forgotten, that my life has been turned upside down.

This time when she left Michel, Pauline gave him a light kiss on the lips.

"In three months," she said, without his being able to guess if this phrase implied a promise.

During those three months, she didn't write, and he didn't think he was allowed to write her.

II

When he found himself alone at La Paix, he practiced his piano, composed a little, leafed through histories of the Cagots, sought out his memories in the little sloping woods, missed the childhood days when he went on endless bike rides with James Warner and other friends. Often he let himself go into a kind of quasi-hypnotic state as he contemplated the Pyrenees. With its mountains and vineyards, it was a landscape not unlike the one that, once upon a time, far from here, had offered itself to his dear Schubert, that eternal walker. Time stopped. Or rather it seemed to.

When the Ossau peak was covered in snow, he remembered an anecdote his mother used to tell:

"Around 1906, 1907—in any case, when I was barely twenty and not yet married—I met a Belgian. He was a cellist at the Winter Palace. He opened a workshop on the Rue Mulot to manufacture skis! He was a true pioneer!"

A peasant woman who came to clean the house spoke from time to time in the local dialect, and Michel enjoyed trying to answer her.

He thought often of Pauline, who had taken on such an enormous importance by giving him so little. As for Monique, he met with her once a week in the café. He looked forward to these meetings with an impatience that surprised him. Monique had asked him not to say a word about their meetings to Jean when he went to the barber. Michel had asked why. Was there anything between them? No, nothing, Monique had protested. But that kind of guy was permanently jealous, that's the way it was. She insisted. "He has no rights over me."

"And if he sees us in the café?"

"I'll tell him we met by accident, that you invited me for a drink to talk about Christophe."

One day she announced that she was going to be away. After hesitating to tell him anything, she ended up revealing that she was going into the hospital for some minor surgery. He asked how he could find out how she was doing. As far as she knew, she would be in a room without a phone. As soon as she was better, she would try to call him. She preferred he not come to see her in the hospital. He wondered if, there again, she wasn't afraid he would find himself face-to-face with Jean. He wanted to insist, but she changed the subject by explaining how during this period a neighbor would take care of Christophe.

She didn't call him until she was back home. It had gone fine. A few days of convalescence and she would be back to normal. He offered to come visit her, and she started to make a fuss, as always with sincere humility. "You mustn't go to any trouble for me."

She lived on the north side of town on the third floor of a house built after the war. Michel brought her a record, Schubert's Sonata for Arpeggione and Piano. In the living room there was an upright piano, a record player, a glassed-in bookshelf with a few books and knickknacks on it, a black vinyl couch, and some Moroccan cushions. He didn't notice any photos of the paratrooper.

"It's nice here, don't you think?" said Monique. "I have to confess something. My parents were Spaniards from the Hédas . . . So you can imagine . . ."

She sighed deeply, a measure of what this revelation had cost her. The Hédas was a sordid ravine that traversed the city, and an impoverished population had still been entrenched there at the time of Monique's birth. Since then it had been subject to "urban renewal," and one could even find fashionable restaurants there now.

"And I," said Michel, "I come from a family of Cagots."

But she didn't know what that was, and he put off his lecture about the Gézitains.

The convalescent didn't seem to feel the effects of her operation. She was dressed to go out. She was even wearing high heels. She offered him a whisky and, as was her custom, served herself an orange juice. They looked over the records in her collection. While Michel made comments about the various works and performers, she said, "I don't dare, but I'd like to take notes."

She had accompanied him to the door. She wanted to kiss him good-bye. But she stayed in his arms and surrendered her mouth. Her lips seemed to change form, as if she didn't kiss with their exterior but with their inner surface, cool and wet. They came back toward the living room holding hands. Standing in the middle of the room, they started again, kissing and caressing each other. Monique let herself slide onto the carpet. Her skirt bunched up; she helped Michel slip off her stockings and panties. And she pulled at his belt buckle. Suddenly there was a noise in the entryway. "It's Christophe," whispered Monique. They got up and straightened their clothes.

"We're acting like high school kids," she said.

Michel went to sit at the piano, or rather he rushed to it and threw himself on the piano bench, barely avoiding a fall. And she, on the couch with her hands on her knees, pretended to listen to him.

Soon afterward it was she who came one evening to the house in the Vallée Heureuse. Offering her lips, she apologized. "I smell of liquor."

"You usually don't drink."

"I wanted to work up my courage."

She toured the house, the garden, admired the city lights in the distance. As they were coming back into the house, she said, "I shouldn't have come. I know what is going to happen. I am going to fall in love with you. And someone like you can't love me. You're going to have fun with me for a while, then you'll leave me. And you'll hurt me."

He didn't know how to reply to the too lucid words except to kiss her and protest. "I would never want to hurt you."

She went to look at the piano, the scores. She asked, "Play some music I've never heard."

He chose from among his records Gesualdo's *Responsories* and gave her a little lecture about the prince-assassin who had composed this angelically suave piece of music. They were seated side by side, and for a moment she pretended to listen. Soon she took one of his hands and began to caress each finger in an almost professional manner. Again her mouth opened, and he rediscovered the kiss from the other day. He held her close to him. But when he started to undo a few buttons, she pulled away.

"I undress alone."

She got up and went to the bedroom. When he joined her, she was in bed with the sheets up to her chin. He made a move to uncover her, but she pleaded with him. "No, don't look at me! Christophe's birth damaged me. He was so big, so strong!"

Yet when he could see her, he found her body charming, almost juvenile, her pubic hair set low. He asked her to stay the night. It was imperative that she go home. Christophe again. He told himself it was an easy excuse.

When she was leaving, sitting at the wheel of her car with the motor already running, she said gravely, "Je vous aime."

For an instant in bed, she had used the informal "tu." Now she was calling him "vous" again, almost with respect.

12

When Pauline came back, he asked her how it had gone at the castle or the prison — he wasn't sure what he was supposed to call it.

"Some other time you should come with me," she said. "It would be a marvelous place for you to work, to compose. There is an excellent piano, and the library contains some old scores that would be worth examining. There may be treasures . . . I am sure that Ugo would be happy if you came and spent time in Bavaria. You could certainly abandon your students for a few weeks."

She concluded with the usual, "Tell me what's new with you."

"Nothing. Nothing has happened. In your absence I entertained myself by imagining what our life would be like if we were married to each other. We would tour the world giving recitals. The renowned Pauline Becker and her accompanist, Michel Mailhoc. But no, what an idiot I am. Your name in that case would not be Pauline Becker."

"Why do you say such things? To make me even sadder to have given up my career ten years ago. Do you hear me? Ten years!"

Michel tried another approach. Quoting *Der Rosenkavalier,* which she loved so, he said, " 'The field marshal is in the Croatian forest, where he is hunting bears and lynx.' Ugo isn't here; let me love you."

A very blonde woman with straight hair cut in the style of the brunette Louise Brooks walked into the music room. She must have been about forty-five years old, but she had maintained the hairdo, the makeup, and the look she must have adopted in her adolescence. The color of her clothes was certainly calculated to emphasize the Nordic lightness of her hair and her eyes. A pale blue silk shirt billowed over her tiny breasts. The young girl she had once been refused to disappear to make way for the woman of today, and this created two superimposed images. Pauline introduced her: "My friend Bernadette, the creator of the painting."

The aged adolescent sat in on the singing lesson while she sketched. The musicians worked on *A Woman's Love and Life*. Michel told Pauline he was sorry not to have known her a few years earlier, in 1956 when he tried to organize an homage to Schumann on the occasion of his centenary. In any case, with or without Schumann, he was sorry not to have known her sooner.

From then on most of the time, instead of the desired tête-à-tête, Michel had to put up with the presence of Bernadette. The two friends joked together, laughing like schoolgirls. Pauline's silences, her sadness, had disappeared. Michel felt excluded, frustrated.

"Don't you find her charming?" Pauline asked with her most innocent look one day when he was able to stay alone with her and complain. "I thought you would like her, that she would make a perfect girlfriend for you."

He retorted dryly, "If I need a woman to console me, you're not the person I'll ask to find me one."

For the moment his consolation was Monique, although when he left Pauline's, she seemed a bit drab. She was younger than Madame Becker, but she had lost her bloom more quickly. No matter how much Michel told himself he had no right to blame her, that it was social injustice creating a gap between the rich and the poor, still . . . On the contrary, when she was in his bed, when they were making love and she called out his name in a voice suddenly gone hoarse, it was Pauline who seemed to him as fake and conventional as a carnival doll. In the end, wasn't that what she was, the beautiful doll who glimmered under the lights of the midway, and no matter how many tickets are bought over and over again, no one ever wins her.

Just as Pauline would say, "Tell me what's new," one of Monique's leitmotifs was "How are your loves?" He used to respond by saying he didn't know what she was talking about. She added, "Sure, with all your students . . ." One day when he had replied, "And you, a pretty manicurist, you must have plenty of clients who proposition you," she responded, "Jean keeps an eye on me."

Now she was agreeing to undress in front of him. One day she arrived with a thin chain around her waist, fastened tight against her skin. He asked her why.

"Don't you understand?"

13

Pauline ran her fingers gently through Michel's hair. A caress or nearly so.

"Don't you think it's too long? You should go to the barber. Unless you've decided to let it grow, to be artsy."

"I haven't had time."

The truth was he didn't want to see Jean anymore, given Monique's constant warnings about him. When he saw the manicurist again, he asked her, "Don't you think I ought to change barbers?"

"Why? Are you jealous?"

"You always told me that he was the jealous one."

"It's not exactly jealousy. I think the guy is dangerous. In any case, he's going to leave the salon soon. He has other plans."

"So then what should I do?"

"Whatever you want. He doesn't know we're seeing each other. If he acts surprised when you don't come back, I'll play dumb."

Monique began to talk about her husband.

"Maybe you think I'm not a despondent enough widow. You know, life with Fabrice was nothing but a series of deceptions. It started the moment we were married. We went on a honeymoon in Andernos on the Bay of Arcachon. As soon as we got there, he said he was bored, and he phoned a few of his friends to come join us. Another paratrooper and his girlfriend. We didn't have a second more of intimacy. On the beach, in the boat, at the restaurant. In the evening, we had to go to a nightclub. Fabrice and his friends drank a lot and wanted to make me drink. It made me sick.

You understand, it was the beginning of my pregnancy. We hadn't waited to be married. That was in fact the reason we got married. One night when they were all drunk in our room, his friend started to feel me up. As for my husband, he was busy with Rosine, the girlfriend. Suddenly I realized they had disappeared. The friend ended up throwing me on the bed and lying flat on top of me. Fortunately— if you can put it that way—I started to vomit. That was my honeymoon."

Michel Mailhoc talked about himself with Monique just as with Pauline. He talked about the legend of Nicolau Arderiu. For these women who hadn't known the Catalan maestro, Michel, who had been so close to him, kept alive a part of the musician's martyred aura. For the rest he varied his speech, adapting it to the woman at hand, only revealing one aspect of himself to each of them. Isn't that what everyone does? As for Monique, she was amused by his amorous adventures in Paris when he was at the conservatory, but she got it into her head that he was unfaithful, and she began to repeat, "How are your loves . . . with all your students . . ." For Pauline he willingly played the sentimental chord.

"Did you know that in 1844 Franz Liszt gave a concert in Pau? And whom did he find in the audience, seated in the second row? The Countess of Artigaux, the woman who had once been Caroline de Saint-Cricq, his great adolescent love. The next day he took a carriage and went to see her on the hillside where she was living, just like you. A reunion that had no other function than to permit them to cry over the past and say one last farewell. Caroline was eighteen when she had fallen in love with her piano teacher and when the Count of Saint-Cricq had politely but firmly dismissed the musician."

"Yet another story of a teacher and a student. You might say Arderiu. Or someone I know."

"Go ahead, mock me! Caroline confessed to him that she was unhappy, that she always had been. She lived another thirty years. Imagine those thirty years! In remembrance of that day on our hillside, Liszt composed a lied, "Ich möchte hingehen wie das Abendrot"—"I would like to disappear like the sunset."

"We should learn it."

"Good idea. We'll make it our song, our rallying cry."

14

 When he passed through town, Ugo Becker wanted to sit in on one of Pauline and Michel's sessions. They were studying the *Kindertotenlieder* in an arrangement in which a piano replaced the orchestral accompaniment. When they had finished, he went to get them a drink. With no warning, no preliminary compliments, he threw out a suggestion: "You wouldn't want to give a recital?"

Pauline protested. She had renounced her career once and for all.

"You'll do what you like," said Ugo Becker. "I am not Citizen Kane, torturing his wife by forcing her to sing opera. It simply gave me pleasure to hear you, and I would like to share this pleasure with my friends."

The idea took shape: a private recital at their home.

During the following weeks Pauline and Michel put the finishing touches on an eclectic program that included romantic lieder as well as melodies by Duparc and Fauré, not to mention Franz Liszt's lied. But as the date approached, the vocalist grew hoarse, then practically lost her voice.

"You're having a psychosomatic reaction; it's stage fright," Michel said.

Nothing reassured Pauline. Overcome with panic, she already imagined that she had contracted throat cancer "like Kathleen Ferrier." Then her laryngitis went away as quickly as it had come.

One evening in January the guests' cars lined up on the lawn that served as a parking lot. Their headlights shone on the grass, giving it a garish green color. The marble palace grew lively, and it didn't seem very different from the receptions the Beckers usually gave. Only they had placed rows of gold chairs in the music room. Michel had worn his tails and thus felt doubly ill at ease.

The guests drank champagne until they were called to the recital. Pauline Becker was wearing a faded red dress with moiré overtones, cut low, showing her bare shoulders. She stood under the large portrait that Bernadette Lanner had never finished finishing. The red in her dress and the red in the portrait didn't go together very well. The recital was a success, and this was because of more than the esteem or good manners of the audience. For an encore the musicians performed Mahler's *Erinnerung*. "Die Liebe weckt die Lieder, die Lieder wecken die Liebe," sang Pauline. "Love calls for song, but song, in turn, calls for love." If only those words could influence her, if only it could be true . . .

The recital was followed by supper. The guests served themselves at a buffet and sat where they liked at little tables. Michel was lost, surrounded by people who bored him. He knew almost no one. Pauline was far away in another room. He decided not to linger, and as soon as it seemed decent, he took leave of his neighbors. The coats were piled in a bedroom on the second floor. As he was climbing the stairs, he was joined by Pauline. She followed him into the bedroom.

"Thank you," she said. "I owe you so much!"

She came to him, and this time she gave him a real kiss. He held her in his arms and gently, as gently as he could, he made her fall backward on the bed, among the coats and furs. He was on top of her, caressing her shoulders, her breasts, her legs. With her low-cut dress, it was easy to plunge his hands in front; easy too under the full red gown to make his way up the length of her black stockings. Pauline let him and continued to give him her mouth. Then they got hold of themselves. The door wasn't closed; anyone could come in.

"What craziness!" Pauline said.

In any case, thought Michel, tangled up in this get-up

with its vest, its tails, and the rest, I didn't quite know how
to proceed. He was in love, unhappy, frustrated, but part
of him found the situation comic.

"Come to my house," he said. "Promise me you'll come."

Pauline kissed him one last time; then she escaped.

15

 Monique's mother and stepfather had come to visit her briefly from the Gard.

On this occasion she launched into a complicated and scarcely believable story. She suspected that her mother's second husband was her true father. They had always known each other, and this man was very close to the family.

"My father, I mean my official father, never showed any interest in me. He never set me on his lap; he didn't kiss me. Whereas the other one was always very affectionate to the point where it embarrassed me."

She had questioned her mother, who was evasive and didn't want to answer.

Michel was barely listening to her. His thoughts were elsewhere, that is, with Pauline.

Finally she announced her visit. That day he canceled his lessons. Pauline Becker arrived in the afternoon behind the wheel of a little car. But she wasn't alone. She had arranged to be accompanied by her friend Bernadette Lanner.

In keeping with the feeling that overwhelmed Michel, the sky was gray.

"It's a day for listening to César Franck," he said.

He remembered fleetingly Nicolau Arderiu's diatribes against the composer of *Redemption*.

Bernadette Lanner suggested, "I really ought to paint your portrait. With the Vallée Heureuse as my background."

He responded almost rudely that he didn't like the way he looked.

"Try to persuade him," Bernadette Lanner said to Pauline, who shrugged her shoulders.

As she was leaving, Pauline noticed a big linden tree at one end of the garden. She cried out, "Der Lindenbaum!"

Softly she sang a passage of the song from *Winter's Journey*.

Ich träumt' in seinem Schatten
So manchen süssen Traum.
Ich schnitt in seine Rinde
So manches liebe Wort;
Es zog in Freud und Leide
Zu ihm mich immer fort.
[In its shade I dreamt
so many sweet dreams.
In its bark I carved
so many tender words;
in joy and sorrow
I was constantly drawn to it.]

Suddenly more prosaic, she told Michel she envied him for being able to make linden tea.

"You will never make me drink a glass of linden tea," he protested. "I'd feel I was gravely ill."

"There's one of your really preposterous ideas! Linden tea is not a medicine. When the tree blooms, it grows fragrant! Will you invite me to come pick its flowers?"

As she got into the car, she announced, "I'm going to spend the rest of the winter in Marrakech."

She added, as if she were giving alms, "I'll be back in May."

16

 The very primitive gears of hygrometers are made out of hair. A woman's hair? One day as he was watching the little chalet carved in wood, the idea came to him that the two dolls symbolized rather well Monique and Pauline. When one withdrew, it was the other's turn. He gave to the blue one the identity of Pauline and to the pink that of Monique. Just as in those regions that the locals themselves call "the wet south," where the weather is often humid and rainy, the blue figurine, the woman with a parasol, was often anxiously expected, awaited, desired, but practically inaccessible. The pink figurine, the one with the umbrella, was very nice but more ordinary, a bit invasive. He resisted the desire to give in to superstition. If the blue doll came out of her hiding place, Pauline would come to him . . . In any case, the hygrometer had seen better days. It was starting to stick. The era of the dolls, the blue one and the pink one, would soon be over.

3

The Victory *of* Time and Disillusion

HANDEL

I

In an antique shop, Michel Mailhoc had found an old adjustable piano stool, which he could set very high. This was in 1940, when the entire family, except for Denis, had taken refuge at La Paix. He had decided to teach his niece, little Pascale, how to play the piano. But the child turned out to be completely rebellious.

Now Edith, Pascale's oldest girl, was five. Remembering that Nicolau Arderiu had started to teach him music at that age, he took out the adjustable stool. The failure was as quick as it had been previously with her mother. The next year with Grégoire, the boy, the same attempt resulted in the same fiasco. Obviously, this branch of the family had no talent.

When Emma, the third child, reached the age of five and he wanted to start again, they made fun of him. He had come over for dinner to talk about it. After having spent the entire evening listening to their jokes and even their ridicule, he finally obtained permission to give it a try.

Soon he came back to fetch Emma. He turned the crank of the piano stool to set the seat as high as possible, a seat made of a faded red velvet that reminded him of Pauline's dress the evening of their recital. And there was Emma, sitting in front of the keyboard.

When he saw this skinny, almost frail little girl place her fingers awkwardly on the keys, her body stiffening with concentration, crinkling up her eyes so that her nose turned up, he was touched and at the same time frightened, as one is when beginning any long journey over time. The pink book of piano exercises was a treacherous trap. If you swallow the bait, if you don't give up like your elder siblings, you don't know for how many years you've condemned yourself to work like a dog, to suffer day after day.

Five years earlier, when Emma was born, he had gone to the movies to see the musical comedy *My Fair Lady,* which had enchanted him. To be a Pygmalion, mold his Galatea. But the poor old Pygmalions are destined to live in fear and trembling, he told himself, as the tunes from *My Fair Lady* rang in his head.

Soon doubt was no longer possible. Emma was talented. Pascale, her mother, made a curious observation. "She isn't like the others. It's because of the egg."

In the building where the Dufresnes lived, there was an old woman at the end of the courtyard who had constructed a farmyard with a bit of wire fencing, though it was a farmyard reduced to a single chicken. When Pascale was pregnant with Emma, she offered her an egg.

"It's very fresh; it will do you good."

Pascale had pricked two holes in the shell and had swallowed the egg.

Shortly afterward when she visited the old lady, she noticed that the chicken, which she had never looked at closely, was a monster. It had three feet. She was terror-struck and told herself that the child she was carrying would be a monster too.

Michel retorted, "In any case, we aren't like others. You know full well we are Cagots."

The rapid progress of the little girl gave him a modest feeling of triumph. When he came to get her, she climbed joyously into the car, cried out when the road began to mount the hillside. Michel let her run around a little in the garden. Then she got down to work with a seriousness he found touching and funny. When she stumbled over a chord, when she didn't manage to overcome a difficulty, she would suddenly become angry.

Often Michel had another student immediately after

Emma, and he couldn't take her home to her parents right away. Instead of going to play in the garden, she sat in on the lesson, her frail body upright, as if she were still sitting at the piano. She never took her eyes off Michel, listening to every last remark he made. When the student left, she would ask, "What about me? When are you going to teach that to me?"

One could never make fun of her because she was so sensitive. Her mother used to say she had a "horrible" temper. Michel had the unfortunate idea of telling her a story. "Once upon a time there was a little boy your age. His name was Mozart. He played the piano so well that all the ladies wanted to kiss him."

Emma started to yell, "I don't want everyone to kiss me!"

Michel asked her who was allowed to.

"My daddy, my mommy, and Laurent."

Laurent was a little friend from school. He came to the Dufresnes often to play with Emma. According to André and Pascale, this child was a total idiot. Why had Emma chosen him?

"Do you love Laurent? Are you in love with him?"

"Yes," the little girl answered gravely.

"What about me? Am I allowed to kiss you?"

"No. You're stupid."

"If you don't love me anymore, I won't give you any more lessons."

Immediately there was despair, weeping, uncontrollable sobs. Michel couldn't forgive himself.

2

 In the end Pauline came back. If one believed her, she couldn't do without Michel. He was the only person who showed her a little affection and filled her with tenderness. But her body was once again inaccessible. She refused him her lips, and she seemed to have forgotten about the evening of the recital, the bedroom where she had fallen backward on the bed covered in clothes. Michel told her that in a salon Chopin amused himself at the piano by improvising musical portraits of the women in the room. When he got to Delphine Potocka, he got up, approached the young countess, took off her shawl, and laid it on the keyboard. He began to play over the cloth. What did he mean by this spectacle? That he had never had the pleasure of undressing Delphine and had to make do with imagining it? Or on the contrary, that he knew her body so well he could describe it simply by running his fingers over the cloth?

As he was telling this, he saw the body of Marie-Christine, sleeping nude in the bungalow on Majorca. But he said, for that was what he was getting at, "And if I were to do your portrait . . ."

Instead of responding, Pauline started to talk about something else.

By now their rehearsals were further apart, and she had lost the habit of her daily telephone calls.

When the perfume of the linden tree began to fill the entire garden, he invited her to come pick its flowers, as she had wished. She replied, "Yes, one of these days," but never came. Michel didn't yet dare admit to himself that in the end, he was bored with her. The day even came when he wasn't unhappy that Bernadette Lanner made a third at their get-togethers. Yet he wasn't interested in Bernadette.

Pauline soon announced that she was going to leave again. This time it was to the music festival in Bayreuth. Bernadette would accompany her. There they would meet up with Ugo and a whole crowd of friends. Why didn't Michel come with them? What an *ursus pyreneus* he was! Since the time she had begged him to come to Bavaria, where he could work in peace and quiet, in the castle . . .

But Michel felt alienated from any plan for a trip or a party. The word "crowd" was all it took to trigger in him that old feeling of being excluded.

"I don't like Wagner."

Which wasn't even true, and he taught his students that one must never reject anything, that one must try to understand everything and perhaps to love everything.

The summer was becoming gloomy. Even little Emma left him to spend the vacation with her grandparents in Antibes.

3

 Monique, who usually talked so much, expressed herself this time with great reluctance. Michel had to drag the whole story from her bit by bit.

"I left the beauty salon."

At first a very vague explanation: "I have other projects."

Then as though it were a detail that had no bearing on her own departure. "Jean too left the shop."

As he encouraged her with questions, she revealed little by little that Jean was going to open a pizzeria near the château, that with the little bit of money she had put aside, she was going to be his partner. With both of them working, there would be fewer overhead expenses. The business was sure to flourish. Because of its good location, it would attract tourists, not to mention young people. Monique kept repeating an expression that was new and which for that reason alone, seemed magical to her. "It's a franchise. Do you know what that is? A franchise?"

"But you hate the guy! You're afraid of him!"

"Yes, but he's a hard worker, a moneymaker. With him a business can't fail. I wasn't going to be a manicurist my whole life! Finally here is a chance I never dreamed of, to own my own business. And you want me to be choosy?"

Then she changed her tone and clung to him. "I love you. Don't you want to keep me here? It's because you reject me that I have to organize my life all by myself."

4

 Some squirrels set up camps in a tree right near the house. Michel announced the news to Emma, and she got in the habit of watching for them, wildly happy whenever they performed their acrobatics in front of her or dared to come down to the lawn. To encourage them to stay, Michel put up a feeder and filled it everyday with seeds and nuts.

When autumn came, the chestnuts rolled down the slope toward the little woods. The little girl loved to gather them. She filled her pockets, her music satchel with them.

"To do what?" Michel said.

She remained mysterious.

She always placed two or three of them, the most beautiful of her harvest, on the piano. They stayed there until they began to shrivel up, until their shells, varnished and veined like precious wood, lost their shine.

The chestnut season didn't last long. For several more weeks Emma was determined to find a few forgotten nuts, hidden under dead leaves. Then she had to admit it was over.

In November in Pau the Saint-Martin's fair takes place on the Haute-Plante. After the lesson and before taking her home to her parents, Michel took Emma for a ride on the carousel. Throughout his entire childhood, he too had waited for November, for this carnival.

"Before, when I was your age, there was a Pierrot dressed in black, who ran a lottery."

"That's not true. Pierrots are white. 'Do do do ré mi ré, do mi ré ré do. Au clair de la lune, mon ami Pierrot.'"

No use insisting.

One year, when the month of September came, Michel announced to the little girl, "The first chestnuts have fallen."

"That doesn't interest me any more," she said.

She wasn't yet ten.

During this period Michel was losing sleep. He was afraid of making a mistake. What he said or did would affect Emma her whole life.

Finally he spoke to her. To focus her attention on the seriousness of the moment, he said, "We are going to have a conversation man to man," which filled her with joy. But next he became completely serious. Weighing his words, he explained that in his opinion, she was doubtless capable of becoming a great pianist. She had what it took. But he could be wrong. Besides which everything, or almost everything, depended on her. It would take perseverance, relentlessness, constant sacrifice. And she could still fail. Because a good part of it was luck. Did she want to commit herself? And if she did, would she find the courage day after day?

"I see it all," said Emma. "I will be a pianist."

Her parents still had to be convinced.

"When will you tell them?" the little girl asked.

It happened one night in May, right after the semirevolution of 1968. Michel was having dinner at the Dufresnes'. Emma had eaten alone earlier and was making the rounds of the dinner table to say good night.

"We'll have to change the schedule of your lessons," Pascale said. "Because of catechism. In a month it's your first Communion."

That's when Emma piped in.

"I am not going to take my Communion."

Her parents were speechless. André Dufresne finally asked why.

"Religion no longer interests me."

Like chestnuts.

"I see that dissent is spreading to the grade schools," said André. "But that's fine. We won't force you."

"Besides," Emma continued, "I have other things to do." She turned toward Michel. "You tell them."

If the idea of Communion had been easily abandoned, the notion that music lessons were to follow a more intensive rhythm and take precedence over schoolwork was less appealing.

"And if all your pipe dreams come to nothing, she'll find herself empty-handed. An illiterate!"

Michel remembered these explanations much later, when Emma sent him letters full of mistakes from the four corners of the world.

This first encounter was followed by several difficult meetings. Once again Pascale called her daughter a monster and remembered the story of the egg from the chicken with three feet, the egg that, to the misfortune of all, she had swallowed while she was expecting this unfortunate child. Michel was a crazy old man. She accused him of having given the girl a big head. He kept saying, "But after all, your grandfather was a musician! Your grandmother was a musician! Weren't they honorable people? Even I . . ."

"You! You used to play in bars! And now you want to turn Emma into a bohemian!"

"And you, you want to turn her into a conformist, whereas her ancestors are Cagots, not to mention the mutineer, the one executed in '17," Michel countered, unafraid to contradict his previous defense of the family's respectability.

The one who was executed in '17 was difficult for André Dufresne to accept. He, the great sportsman, had done his military service as a paratrooper. He forgot to mention that he had finished just in time to avoid the Algerian War.

"I had a sergeant, he really gave us a hard time. Sergeant Gérard! It's too bad girls don't get drafted! Someone like him would have whipped her into shape!"

So André Dufresne had been under the command of Monique's husband. If he could imagine the rest! To play the devil, Michel amused himself by declaring, "I've heard of this Sergeant Gérard. He was killed in Algeria."

Emma did not always take part in these painful sessions. But one day when she was there, shut off in her silence, absent, as if the fate being decided weren't hers, there was for a brief instance an exchange of glances between her and Michel. Their eyes said that they were alone against the world. The two of them. And that this feeling was strong enough to allow them to hold firm against the others or at least to ignore them and feel happy about it.

5

 Motivated by curiosity, Michel went to the neighborhood of Henri IV's château near the pizzeria. He approached it cautiously. Posted on the sidewalk across the street, slightly hidden, he could see the inside of the shop. Monique was alone behind the counter. She was wearing a white apron and on her hair, sitting coquettishly to one side, a little white cap with a red border. A door in the back must have led to the kitchen. In the shop a few tables awaited anyone who wanted to eat there. For the time being, there was no one. He crossed the street and entered. The smell of warm dough surrounded him. Monique looked upset.

"Go away," she said. "Don't stay here."

She made a gesture that perhaps meant Jean was in the back room.

"Plus," she added, "I don't like you seeing me in this outfit."

There was nothing to do but beat a retreat.

"Don't come back."

But she corrected this ban with an apology and reminded him that she was coming to his house the next night.

6

May '68 frightened Ugo Becker. He decided to sell the marble palace. According to him, France was an impossible country where one was never sure of anything. Michel Mailhoc understood that Pauline was going to disappear from his life. They had one last, quite absurd, or rather completely open discussion, since their words no longer committed them to anything.

"I was tempted to leave with you," Pauline said. "But you mustn't have regrets. You wouldn't have been happy with me. I'm too depressive."

"Ugo told me one day that you were incapable of loving. That's why he wasn't jealous of me."

"He doesn't know me. But I thought you did at least a little. Incapable of loving! If you knew . . ."

"When Ugo says he isn't jealous, I'm not so sure. Is it possible he'd sell this house and take you far away from here because of me?"

Pauline replied that she didn't think that was at all true, which was a bit humiliating. She concluded coquettishly. "You'll forget me right away. There are so many women, your students, the mothers of your students . . ."

And then the Parthian shot, as it's called since the Parthians would fire on you as they fled: "It seems there's a very common woman in your life, a hairdresser, someone like that."

As they exchanged these words, they were seated next to each other, and she took his hands, an unusual gesture that ended in reciprocal caresses, their fingers separating to wander on each other's wrists and arms. Pauline was wearing a short dress, and Michel lay his hand on her knee.

"Don't arouse me," she said.

She got up. At the moment of their farewell, she gave him the most passionate kiss he had ever received from her. He held for a few moments the body of this woman who, in that moment, he was sure he had loved deeply. His hands discovered her shoulders, the small of her back, the weight of her breasts, but it was definitely too late.

7

Emma rummaged in the pocket of her jeans. She took out a golf ball.

"Here," she said to Michel. "It's for you."

She explained that she had gone for a walk with some girlfriends near the golf course at Bilhères beyond the grounds of the château, and that they had looked for lost golf balls in the bushes. She made a business of it, selling them to a junk dealer at the flea market. Michel thanked her and, playing the great-uncle for once, told her he didn't much like this trafficking. The golf ball found a home in an ashtray on the piano.

This was nothing, it's true, compared with the worries that Monique had with her son. One evening she had arrived at Michel's completely undone. Christophe had given her a large radio with a tape deck. At the time she had wanted to refuse it. First of all, where had he gotten the money? He could claim all he liked that he was doing odd jobs after school. (He was waiting impatiently to turn sixteen so he wouldn't have to go anymore.) But since for once he had made a kind gesture toward her, she thought it unwise to discourage him. And the next day a big headline in the newspaper announced the robbery of a well-known appliance store in town. It was blamed on a gang. So Christophe was part of a gang! In despair she waited for Michel to advise her.

"If I turn in the radio, I'm denouncing my son. If I keep it, I'm guilty of concealing evidence."

What to say? What to do? Michel advised her to have it out once and for all with Christophe and throw the radio in the trash. He asked her if she had discussed this with her partner.

"With Jean? Are you crazy? He hates Christophe, and I don't trust him. He isn't legitimate himself."

From then on, Monique no longer mentioned the episode. With her a new drama always erased the previous one. Suddenly she wondered if she had cancer. This was something she had in common with Pauline Becker. Michel tried several times to ask her about it. Her responses weren't very clear. Most likely she had kept the tape player. But since it was she who came to La Paix—he didn't go to her house because of her son—he couldn't know for certain.

Was it to cut his questioning short? She threw herself at him, begging him, "Love me! Protect me! You don't love me!"

He was accustomed to the thin chain she wore around her hips, symbol of her dependence, hidden from all eyes, visible only to the one she had chosen as her master.

8

 In the morning while making coffee, he would listen to the news. One day when he didn't turn off the radio immediately after the headlines, he heard a song that was announced as the latest hit. It was impossible to tell if the voice was a boy's or a girl's. He was about to turn off the sound when it struck him that this tune reminded him of something. After a moment he recognized it. At the same time, he didn't want to believe his ears. It was the funeral ode that Nicolau Arderiu had written for his personal use. Almost unrecognizable, transformed into a syrupy melody mixed with violent rock music. This is what Florence had permitted! He was all the more indignant since he had contacted her again by letter quite some time ago, when he had gotten it into his head to publish Nicolau Arderiu's complete works. She had been careful not to tell him about this adaptation.

Emma, who was twelve, was in a phase of infatuation with rock music. Michel didn't like it at all, even though he knew he was out-of-date. He, at least, had liked good jazz.

"Listen carefully," he told her.

He played Arderiu's funeral ode.

"Do you recognize this piece?"

Emma knit her eyebrows.

"It could be, 'If you go to Woodstock, put a flower on my tomb . . .' or some song like that. But you're playing it like a dolt. You have no rhythm."

"Thank you."

Michel thought suddenly that he was nearly the same age as Nicolau Arderiu when he was taken hostage and disappeared forever.

9

Monique's dramas took a new turn. She started to complain about "not getting by." Michel asked her if the pizzeria was doing badly. She claimed that Jean Renucci gave her hardly any money. It was impossible to see the books. Besides, she didn't understand. It was true that they didn't have many customers. And Jean didn't seem interested in his business. He let it drop at the least whim. But at times his pockets were full of cash. He spent it like it was nothing. When she asked for some, he threatened her. He drank and got angry like an alcoholic.

"The truth is that he's in love with me. And since I want nothing to do with him, he takes it out on me."

Soon afterward Michel happened to come upon a magazine article, explaining how certain small businesses — boutiques, appliance stores, cheap jewelry shops, or pizzerias — in fact served to launder money earned illegally by bank robbers, pimps, drug dealers. Since customers usually paid in cash in that type of establishment, it was easy to disguise illicit gains against receipts. And if the fictional earnings were in danger of looking suspect, it seemed it was child's play to prove there were corresponding purchases, thanks to fake bills produced by "instant companies."

The article was enlightening. Monique's abominable partner must be linked to the mob, and his pizzeria should have been called a laundry. He tried to explain to his girlfriend what he had figured out. He was not at all certain she believed him. He urged her, in any case, to break off her partnership with this guy. She responded immediately that it wasn't possible. Jean would refuse to give her back her share. And afterward, even if she did get back part of it, what would she live on?

"I'm certainly not going to become a manicurist again!"

To tear herself away from her former profession—that was the argument she invoked when Michel would ask her how she could have gotten herself mixed up with a man about whom she always said the worst. But when she proclaimed her hatred for the former hairdresser, was she always completely sincere, or was she not exaggerating a little? And why? Out of her penchant for storytelling, or to please Michel because she thought he was jealous? She sketched the portrait of a man so vile and dangerous, Michel told himself if he had the means he would gladly kill him with no scruples whatsoever. He devised plans: catch him in a trap, or wait for him at night and knock him down. Each time, he saw in his imagination a little side street that went down a steep slope from the château to the Place de la Monnaie in the lower part of town. A perfect throat-cutting location. But why would Jean go near there in the middle of the night? Because of this guy, Michel was reconsidering the absolute respect in which he had always held human life.

When he advised Monique anew to break off her relationship, she responded that it would soon take care of itself without her having to intervene. There wouldn't be much more to deal with. She had discovered that Jean was suffering from cirrhosis of the liver. He was a goner. Three months from now perhaps, he would be dead. A doctor had guaranteed it.

She was so sure of herself when she gave in to this kind of mythomania, it was useless to discuss it. Besides which, Michel's first instinct was to believe her.

There was one obvious way to rescue Monique. But Michel had no intention of doing it. She was right when she said, "You don't love me." At least, not enough. Still, he felt guilty watching her founder. Retreating to his house on the hillside, so derisively called La Paix, he felt like a shipwrecked egotist who succeeded in finding dry land on an island while others were still struggling in the eddy and foam of the tides.

This attitude now reigned even in his teaching. He was reacting against Nicolau Arderiu's influence. The Catalan pianist had always practiced his seductive ways on his pupils. He wanted to please. In a word, he was a bit of a whore. Michel found he had imitated him only too much. More and more with his students, he forced himself to be strict, technical.

All that remained were the moments when little Emma was there. He felt so happy then that the countryside, the sky, the hills, and the mountains melted in a luminous harmony.

One night he was woken by the telephone. At first he didn't recognize the thick voice. He heard it calling, "Michel! Michel!"

Finally he recognized Monique. He asked her where she was.

"I don't know."

When he insisted, she said that she had left in her car and that she was somewhere in the Landes on the banks of a lake. He had to extract this information from her in bits. And always that thick voice.

"I'm in a hotel room. I took some pills."

What hotel, what town, she was incapable of telling him. She kept repeating, "A town in the Landes on the banks of a lake." Or else she was just refusing to say more.

"No one knows where I am. You're the only one I called. I wanted to say good-bye, that's all."

She hung up.

What to do? There are so many lakes lined with hotels in the Landes.

He asked directory assistance for the phone number of

the Mont-de-Marsan police. When he got the station, he tried to explain that someone was in danger in a hotel room on a lake. Her name was Monique Gérard. She must have gone there in her car. What kind of car? A Renault 5. Very original! The license number? He couldn't remember it. Blue. All he could say was that it was blue.

"With the information you've given us, we won't get far."

"I thought that the police kept tabs on all the hotels."

"Besides that, there's a chance she registered under an assumed name. And you forget it's two in the morning."

"I beg you, do something!"

"We'll make a few phone calls to Hosegor, to Soustons…"

The Landes is a limbo. One sinks into a fog where the pines, the ferns, the sand, the marshes melt together. Michel loved this region for its monotony, its melancholy. But today that limbo had swallowed up this poor girl. He remembered the unhappy woman who had arranged for Nicolau Arderiu to give piano lessons to her dead son and who had gone off to drown herself in Biarritz. Did Nicolau feel guilty when he received her letter, as Michel did today? Did he blame himself for not having found a way to save a woman in mortal distress?

Monique was found unconscious in Seignosse near the Black Swamp and transported to the hospital in Bayonne. Michel was informed by Christophe, who didn't seem unduly worried. When Michel asked him what he was going to do while his mother was hospitalized, the boy answered with a laconic, "I'll make do."

Michel continued to feel guilty. He knew he was wrong as far as the night of the drama was concerned. What more could he have done? But before?

He went to Bayonne. This time Monique agreed to let him see her in the hospital. As he was looking for her room, they told him "Right, that would be the A.S."

Here Monique was an "A.S." — an Attempted Suicide.

She was installed in a rather pleasant room, and she seemed in a good mood, practically gay. In her bed she looked quite charming. She was wearing a very low-cut black nightie, the one she must have chosen to die in. She welcomed Michel sweetly, and it was she who apologized.

10

 Michel was invited to dinner at the parents of one of his students, and he couldn't get out of it. At their house he met a blonde with long hair. It took him a few seconds to recognize Bernadette Lanner, Pauline's friend.

"I had enough of playing a latter-day Louise Brooks. Besides, even Louise Brooks ended up growing hers out."

He asked her if she'd had any news from Pauline. She didn't know much. Her life continued as always in Becker's shadow.

"You were in love with her, weren't you?"

Bernadette explained her own point of view, which was quite different from what he believed he had understood.

"Despite her moments of revolt, she loves Ugo, and she admires him. The rest is only to pass the time. You mustn't believe her when she says she's angry with Ugo for making her give up her career. On the contrary, he rendered her an enormous service. He allowed her to believe that for love she had given up the possibility of becoming a great soprano, when in fact she was all set to become a little third-rate singer."

So they chatted throughout the evening whenever they could tear themselves away from the other guests.

"You were in love with Pauline," Bernadette Lanner began again, "but there was another woman, one or several."

What was it with the people in this town, wanting to pay attention to him, to gossip about him behind his back? He had just understood that, despite the music and a certain attraction, very few things had tied him to Pauline, whereas she and her husband possessed an entire world in common.

II

When Emma was fourteen, he gave her a moped. He no longer needed to pick her up, and she, for her part, enjoyed a new freedom.

She was old enough for a moped, which meant he had been working with his great-niece for nine years. Almost a decade! The more she progressed, the more intensely determined she became. Michel began to be afraid he wasn't a good enough teacher for her. She would need greater maestros. In any case, for now her parents wouldn't let her leave.

However much an aging man and an adolescent may live side by side, time doesn't pass for them at the same speed. Emma was surely impatient to reach adulthood. As for Michel, he saw her change so quickly that he was terrified. Not so much physically. She had grown taller, but she remained thin and flat. She was still silent, wild, and couldn't have had many friends. Yet her parents complained that since her great-uncle had bought her that moped, they didn't see her anymore. All that was left was for her to fall in love! However many times Michel told himself this was inevitable, in the natural order of things, and that he'd have to make his peace with it when it happened, still it scared him to imagine all that would change.

Now Emma kept cigarettes in her satchel along with her scores. Those autumns were already far away when she had used it to keep her store of chestnuts.

She continued to confront her parents in scenes that sometimes became violent. If Michel was there, they made him feel that they held him in large part responsible for Emma's bad grades, for her carryings-on, her eternally absent look, her silences broken by a few ferociously insolent words. André Dufresne turned out to be more intransigent, more hostile than his wife, who occasionally seemed to understand her daughter. He would quip, "You Mailhocs, you really are one of a kind!"

His two older children consoled him by being good at sports, like he was. Edith and Grégoire were making a name for themselves in regional tennis matches and ski races.

Often the family arguments became confused. Emma clashed with her parents, with Michel's help when he was present. But it sometimes happened that in the midst of an argument, Pascale and André would begin to quarrel with each other. Suddenly Emma was nothing but a pretext, and sometimes she was even completely forgotten. Although fights horrified Michel, he found this satisfying. At one moment or another, there was that exchange of glances through which Emma seemed to be telling him she had no one but him. But did he still have the right to believe she had no one but him?

When she had reached the age at which young people can drive a moped, another adolescent also crossed a threshold. As if events took place in twos or in series—even though Michel found it repugnant to make the slightest comparison between his beloved great-niece and Monique's son, that good-for-nothing who had already sunk into delinquency. Christophe was eighteen. He had come of age. He didn't waste a minute leaving his mother's home to go live with his buddies.

Soon after, Monique came to speak with Michel in an embarrassed tone of voice that he recognized immediately. She had explained with the same hesitation in her voice, the same lowered glance, her departure from the beauty salon, the opening of the pizzeria, her son's theft of the radio.

"Now that Christophe no longer lives with me, I have no more reason to pay this steep rent. You know full well I'm not getting by."

But after this habitual complaint, it was difficult to get her to tell him the rest.

She ended up admitting that Jean, who had a big apartment, had persuaded her to share it with him.

"But each of us can have a place of our own. It divides quite easily."

"Why don't you just tell me you're going to live with him?"

"Are you crazy? I think he's horrible! I couldn't stand him touching me!"

Her denials proliferated. Michel asked her what she could be thinking in knowingly going to live with an alcoholic who was also a gangster. Lacking further arguments, she lashed out: "Maybe I'm doing something stupid. But it's done."

"Didn't you tell me one day that he had cirrhosis of the liver and only had three months left to live? You told me that how long ago? A year? Eighteen months?"

"I was mistaken. Or not me but the doctors."

Monique did in fact move. She stopped coming to see Michel. She hadn't given him her phone number. She wrote him:

Jean has me sequestered. I have the right to go to work at the pizzeria, and afterward I go home with him and he locks me in. He is even viler than I thought. He threatens me constantly. I'm afraid. Don't try to see me. When I talk about you, he goes crazy. How did it come to this? Since you don't want me, I've built myself a prison.

How was he supposed to understand this letter? Was Monique asking him to rescue her, or was she telling him that he was dismissed? He wondered if she had always been lying about Jean, if she hadn't been having an affair with him back in the days of the beauty parlor. It would make the fact that she shared a business with him, then an apartment, more understandable. The gold chain she wore under her clothes around her hips was perhaps not a sign of voluntary submission to Michel, as she claimed, but more likely was imposed upon her by Jean Renucci. When she described the burial of her husband in the Gers, she tried to win sympathy by reporting how her father-in-law had kicked her out the door, calling her a tart. And if the old man was right?

From there, Michel thought of Pauline, who also used to say that she was sequestered in her distant castle.

Paul Dukas, a musician who closed himself off in silence for nearly a quarter century, wrote about his opera, *Ariane and Blue Beard:* "No one wants to be released."

Michel made one attempt to see Monique at the pizzeria. This time a couple of customers were seated at a table near the window for a view of the château. Monique was wearing her uniform, her little white cap tilted to one side across her hair, American style. As she went to take their order, she noticed him in the street. She made a violent gesture with her hand to drive him away, and he didn't insist.

12

 Emma was fifteen when her parents separated and decided to divorce. The two older children, the jocks, stayed with their father. Emma went to live in a small apartment with Pascale. The mother and daughter had in common the fact that they were two silent women. But everything that in the daughter was concentration, high standards, intense inner life had become in the mother refusal, negation. Pascale settled into the unhappiness of having been rejected by her husband. Soon after the divorce, André Dufresne remarried. Michel was gradually becoming the adolescent's only support and only guide. Without ever having put it into words, her parents seemed to look to him to assure the future of the girl, whom he had chosen from childhood as his pupil and whom he had drawn into a risky career. One day when she was in a more bitter mood than usual, Pascale snapped at Michel, "You've taken my daughter from me."

13

 Michel avoided the pizzeria. At the end of a few months, finding himself near the château, he gave in to a desire he had had for a long time, and he approached it. He didn't intend to go in, only to see the place and perhaps to get a glimpse of Monique. But the pizzeria wasn't there anymore. He thought he had the wrong block or the wrong building. He finally figured out it had been replaced by a shop selling souvenirs, postcards, Basque linens, candy, and the inevitable dolls dressed as paratroopers. He went in. The salesman knew nothing about the previous owners.

He remembered that in the article he had read about laundering ill-gotten money, which had made him suspect that Jean Renucci's business was not on the up and up, they had spoken of "lightning shops," too ephemeral to be tracked down.

14

Michel glanced angrily at the linden tree. He felt the same way every year when it grew fragrant. He'd remember Pauline's defection, the flowers she had never come to pick. Then he'd reason with himself. He wasn't going to chop down that fine old tree on account of a woman. "Es zog in Freud und Leide / Zu ihm mich immer fort" — In joy and sorrow / I was constantly drawn to it.

And then too every year at this time, when the press and the radio would report on the festival in Bayreuth, he'd think to himself that Pauline must be there, surrounded by her court. He couldn't help but dream about the past. Not that the present was completely empty. Only he found it of little importance. The time of the great flames was over. What was left was the brushfire, so quickly extinguished.

He was increasingly bothered by self-doubt and didn't know if he alone was capable of guiding Emma, his student, to the heights. It was so hard to capture the essence of an art both sensual and mathematical, manual and intellectual! When she was eighteen, he persuaded her to take master classes at the Accademia Musicale Chigiana in Siena. She said she would do it on one condition: that he accompany her. Of course, nothing could have made him happier.

At the Chigi-Saracini Palace in Siena, the greatest musicians teach students from all corners of Europe and America, not to mention Japan. They are admitted on the strength of their achievements or selected by audition. Emma got in with no difficulty. The palace on the Via di Città had the aura of a magic place. One had only to enter the courtyard, where there was a well and another vaulted inner courtyard decorated with a fresco, sit there on the stone bench, and capture fleetingly the gusts of music coming from each window. As for the rooms where the classes were held, they were former salons with high ceilings, gold-leafed woodwork, and paintings—good and awful—from every era, landscapes from seicento and 1930s society portraits in a happy jumble all over the walls. Utterly impractical rooms, in other words, and utterly charming. From top to bottom the palace was filled with boys and girls. Michel asked himself once more what he was doing there.

Among the agreeable confusion of paintings, one of them caught Michel Mailhoc's attention or rather made him hear the voice of Nicolau Arderiu. It depicted an orchestra of angel musicians playing antique instruments. Arderiu used to tell how during the Tang dynasty, the poet Wang Wei, who was also a great painter and a great musician, found himself standing one day in front of a painting of instrumentalists. He said, "They are in the middle of playing the first measure of the third refrain of the *Dance of the Rainbow Gowns*."

Musicians were summoned. At the first measure of the third refrain, they held the exact positions of the people in the painting.

Emma seemed very happy. She was working with a famous Spanish pianist who had heard tell of the Arderiu dynasty. So he wanted to meet Michel Mailhoc—who was anxious to hear what he would have to say about his student.

"Don't think that I'm speaking lightly. She reminds me of Clara Haskil. Petite, fragile, and capable of demonstrating a will of iron, just like her. But more often, and this is the best thing about her, she opens her heart and creates a pensive, poetic music. Her slow movements in particular are like a lament, sung quietly, so melodious that they calm the soul. It is a sweet and sad way to speak of love.

Then as soon as the allegro returns, violence is beneath her fingers again."

There was also the extraordinary master class given by a celebrated artist. For three hours he did nothing but explain sixteen measures of Beethoven's Sonata no. 18 in E-flat. To those sixteen measures he brought the whole of music and the whole history of his life as a musician. Emma walked out of this class overwhelmed.

She made friends almost right away. At first she ate her meals with Michel in the pensione where they were staying. Then more and more she would go to lunch or dinner with other students. There was an Austrian who wouldn't leave her alone. Michel was obliged to notice, and he allowed himself to make only one extremely cautious remark, knowing that ever since she was a child, Emma had shown him how touchy and how attached to her independence she was.

She responded, "He is the worst student in the piano class. He gets yelled at all the time, and we laugh at his expense. I feel sorry for him."

"If you begin like that, mistaking pity for love, you'll never see the end of it," said Michel.

She shrugged one thin shoulder.

Much as he might joke, the moment when she would take flight, detach herself from him to choose a true accomplice — the moment he had started to fear the very day of her first lesson, when he had jacked up the piano stool as high as it could go, picked up the five-year-old little girl by the waist with his two hands and set her down in front of the keyboard — that moment was here, and it had come along so naturally in its own good time that it was absurd and a bit disgusting to be affected by it.

For a solitary tourist, Siena was not lacking in attractions. Michel didn't care much for museums. The Virgins in Sienese paintings, with their stooped look, annoyed him. He was content to wander the streets, watch the people from the terrace of a café on the Piazza del Campo. He did go, however, to the San Domenico Church when he learned that Catherine of Siena's head was on display there. He stood for a long time in front of the glass shrine, fascinated by that dried-up face, which had been detached from the body to be balanced on the top of this altar, a stone's throw from the chapel where she had experienced her ecstasy. The body in Rome, the head in Siena. Beneath the empty yet terrifying gaze of Catherine Benincasa, he began to dream of lost loves.

Then came the closing recital for the piano class. The students each played their best piece. Emma chose Schumann's *Humoresque* op. 20. Beyond the apparent discontinuity, the shimmering phantasmagoria, there was the intellectual rigor of the composer and, more secretly, his suffering. Michel was against this choice. He thought a little more intellectual maturity was needed, and also perhaps it was necessary to have suffered. Not to mention technique. Emma's triumph left him almost undone. He was moved to the point of tears, but at the same time, annoyed that he had been mistaken.

It was time to go home. Emma asked Michel to return alone to Pau. She wanted to stay two days longer to visit Florence "with friends."

"Say with a friend," Michel reprimanded her. She didn't respond, but asked that he conspire with her. That he not say anything to the family. That once he was back, he play dead for forty-eight hours. Play dead! What a way to talk!

Just as Michel Mailhoc had suspected, the trip to Siena and the study in Chigiano marked the beginning of the young pianist's ascent. Shortly after her return, she left for Paris. Soon she faced the great international competitions. In the Queen Elizabeth of Belgium Competition, she took second honorable mention. This was not what Michel had wished for. Still, it was enough for her to be offered several concerts and radio broadcasts. Next she entered the International Marguerite Long Competition. It took place in mid-December. At La Paix behind his window, Michel looked out at the bare garden, the rose bushes without flowers, the trees without leaves, the chestnut trees in the little woods that the girl had loved so passionately once upon a time, and in the distance the Ossau valley, the Pyrenees covered in snow. He went out, crossed the road, took the slope down toward the woods. If he found one more chestnut under the rotten leaves, Emma would win the competition. He found one, and she was victorious.

Finally there was the International Tchaikovsky Competition, in Moscow. It was the only time that Michel made the trip with her. He was in the audience, and he knew that Emma was waiting her turn in the green room and that an anxious sweat must be running between her shoulder blades. When she appeared, or rather when she slid furtively onto the stage wearing the same black dress as always, it all seemed too big for her—the stage, the piano. She had to play Haydn's Sonata in E-flat Major. When she started the exposition of the first movement and its development, Michel was incapable of hearing a note. He didn't start to gather his wits together until the coda, whose counterpoint he beat silently to himself. Already the adagio was flowing beneath the musician's fingers, a majestic passage dominating the room like a prince distributing his boons. Michel kept thinking, "I'm in Moscow, and it is Emma playing." He wondered if she were as disoriented as he. Probably not. These contests, these trips formed the fabric of her life, which was only beginning. She was light-years from her fabled ancestors: the Cagots, the executed great-grandfather, the great-grandmother who had known Cléo de Mérode. Had she any idea of that war, already so far away, during which her grandfather had been a prisoner, her great-uncle wounded, and the legendary Arderiu deported to a death camp? Michel had never wanted to bore her with stories of the old days. How odd it was on reflection that in France, such a well-preserved country, privileged in comparison with many others, men so close to him had been crushed by history and that, give or take a little, he might have been as well. He came out of his reverie because Emma had begun to attack the dramatic episode in B-flat minor. At last there was the force and the mastery of the final movement.

Emma took first place. After so many laurels, her career as a concert pianist could begin.

15

Baudelaire wrote this enigmatic phrase:
"La Musique creuse le ciel."*

Michel Mailhoc thought of it at night while wandering in the garden. He felt bare and vulnerable. He'd lived most of his life in this countryside, and still, it was only in the heart of a city that he felt protected. On the hillside you were in direct contact with infinity. The Milky Way made him dizzy, as if it were carrying away the fugitive seasons. The proximity of the mountains, invisible, added to his uneasiness.

By day this corner of nature, so appropriately named La Vallée Heureuse — the Happy Valley — became sunny, innocent.

For a long time he used to think that a man was only worth the sorrow he had known. Then he stopped believing this. Suffering isn't a token of anything. During another period he told himself that if he didn't leave behind a body of music, his life and his death would be meaningless. But the more years that passed, the less he was persuaded. All these scores, he didn't know himself if they were mediocre or whether they had remained obscure from lack of ambition, savoir-faire, from negligence. Too polite certainly, not "contemporary" enough. As a performer too in the tradition of Arderiu as much as out of personal taste, he had favored the classical repertoire, and now Emma did too. They were the faithful servants of the piano. They weren't going to abandon it for some electronic machinery that

---

* Baudelaire's phrase could be translated as "music ploughs the sky" or, more lyrically, as "music hollows out the heavens." *Trans.*

makes sound. Being modest, he would have needed reassurance about the value of his music. But from whom?

Now he found a new justification for these staves he had blackened. He read them over the way one looks at a photo album. Each score was tied to a memory. In listening to them mentally, he revisited the episodes of his life with Muriel, Florence, Marie-Christine, Pauline, Monique, and the others. Thus, rereading a sort of slow waltz in D major, he suddenly remembered how, in the big bed of the Freudian bedroom in the center of the spider web, Muriel had risen up above him and pinned his shoulders down, victorious and vanquished. When he was composing, the fluidity, the fervor, the surrender of feminine forms, blended with the rules of musical writing in a unique inspiration.

He tried to remember how it had ended each time. He asked himself naively why these women who had shown a certain passion for him had one day ceased to want to see him.

Following in Arderiu's footsteps, he started to read Nietzsche, or at least the passages where he talks about music. He wanted to apply to himself the cruel words that the philosopher aimed at Brahms, suddenly repudiating him: "He is, in particular, the musician for a certain species of frustrated woman."

Albert Savinio says that *Madame Bovary* could not have been written before the appearance of photography and of the piano. And he, Michel, had his art of the piano been nothing but an instrument of seduction?

16

 Emma arrived one day at La Paix with a puppy, a present for her great-uncle.

"I thought he would make a good companion. And with a garden, he won't give you much work. No need to take him out."

He was a yellow Labrador, whose paws were already big.

"Do you seriously think you can be replaced by a dog? Why not a TV set?"

"If you're going to be like that, I'll take him back!"

The dog was named Frescobaldi, soon shortened to Fresco. Once he was beyond the idiocy of puppyhood, he became an utterly faithful companion, and Michel was surprised by this love given once and for all, unconditionally. Among humankind, he hadn't found anything similar, neither in himself nor in others. He gave Fresco the old golf ball, which became his favorite toy.

After a few years of living together, when they found themselves with a third person the dog and the man began to exchange conspiratorial glances. They can say what they like; it's of little interest to us, and after all, we don't give a damn about them. The same type of look that Michel used to exchange with Emma.

For the piano the young virtuoso still came back to Michel. For technique she certainly no longer needed him. It was but a sort of superstition, he realized. She wanted to be reassured, to share her doubts as she was finishing the preparation of a piece. As long as he hadn't told her that it was good, she couldn't consider herself satisfied. As for the rest, she never asked his advice. At the most, from time to time she offered up a confession in this vein: "I don't know how I manage; I always end up with guys who are impossible."

From indirect sources, Michel learned that she had let one of these guys, terminally unemployed, move in with her, then another who was jealous and who went so far as to slap her around, then still another who was an alcoholic painter. Day after day, it all added up to how many dramas, scandals, tears, about which he knew nothing? There in Paris, so far away.

During the period of the alcoholic painter, he thought of Chopin, so upset when Solange, George Sand's daughter, married that brutal and dishonest man, the sculptor Clésinger: "Soon," wrote Chopin, "we'll be seeing Solange's little derrière in white marble at the Salon."

During one of her visits, Emma suddenly came crying into his arms. "I can't take it any more! I don't know what to do!"

But if he had wanted to intervene, she wouldn't have let him.

If he was distraught by the young woman's disastrous lovers, sometimes too the dark thought occurred to him that the day she found a decent man she wouldn't need him anymore. In any case, every time a new character entered Emma's life, he went three or four days without sleeping. He reasoned with himself in vain: Be fair. I don't tell her everything either. There are entire parts of my life about which she has no idea.

There was the period when she was surprised to see a recording of guitar music lying around his house — the *Popular Brazilian Suite* by Villa-Lobos. He hadn't thought it was a good idea to confide in her that a guitarist had passed through his existence for a few months.

Whatever the dramas of the moment, they never affected Emma's work. She delivered, as they say. She appeared before her public on time. During a concert she replaced her worries and sorrows with that terrible stage fright she had never been able to get over.

When she was twenty-five, she already had a strand of white hair, which, out of a sort of vanity, she refused to have colored.

Sometimes when she appeared before him, the past seized him by the throat. Where was the little girl he used to pick up with his two hands and set down on the old piano stool?

When he couldn't help showing how worried he was about the life she was leading in Paris, he apologized right away. "I sound like an old nursemaid."

She worried too, watching him grow old. "It looks to me like you've lost more weight!"

For diversion and to banish those black thoughts, they had invented a game, the audition game. Emma had come to introduce herself to a most illustrious orchestra conductor to see if he would accept her as a soloist. Michel Mailhoc played the conductor. While she started to play the piano part of Brahms's First Concerto, he hummed the orchestra's responses, all the while mimicking Karajan, standing up, his eyes closed, his two hands caressing the air slowly, voluptuously, ecstasy and suffering. Another time, grimacing to keep his eyes slanted, all smiles and bows, he was Seiji Ozawa listening to the candidate play Mozart's Piano Concerto no. 21. It always ended with an urgent request from Emma:

"Do Toscanini!"

She played Beethoven's Second Concerto. He pretended to get angry, to tug at his mustache; he had brusque, choppy gestures. He started to run across the room, jumping on one foot, twisting and turning, skidding, losing and miraculously regaining his balance while twirling an imaginary cane. Toscanini became Charlie Chaplin.

Sometimes she asked him to take her to the airport. In an

hour or two she would be in Paris, in another world. Modern times had abolished distance but not yet mental distance. On the road home he was always surprised to see how the city had grown, changed. Arderiu wouldn't recognize it. Sometimes in the solitude of La Paix, he allowed himself to listen to one of Emma's recordings, the *Kreisleriana*. In the second half of the fourth movement, lento assai, it never failed, his eyes filled with tears. Then came a moment when she didn't play exactly the way he would have liked. His tears stopped. Besides, he didn't like Emma's photo on the album cover.

Other times he hummed Gabriel Fauré's *Dolly* because it was one of the first four-handed duets she had played with him, just as he had done with Nicolau Arderiu. A fresh and melancholy air, full of childhood. Sometimes he gave Emma that name, Dolly. In those days he had explained to her that playing a two-piano duet implies a rivalry, whereas playing with four hands on the same keyboard is inconceivable without friendship. That is why Schubert wrote so many pieces for four hands.

Still other times he sat at his piano and played Beethoven's sonata *Les Adieux,* only because it was called *Les Adieux* and because, since he didn't see her as much as he wanted, he wished never to see her again. Or else he put on the hi-fi Schubert's Fantasia in C Major for Violin and Piano, constantly attacked by the critics from its debut for its brusque movements of the heart, in which he found the image of his own. When Emma left him without news for a long period, he composed a little fugue in E minor, E for Emma. There was a principal theme, symbolizing Emma, and a secondary theme, returning again and again, changing moods each time, a chromatic whirl carrying the heroine off and representing her various lovers. He also slipped in, almost surreptitiously, a quotation from Schubert, taken from the first movement of the unfinished Sonata in E Minor. Schubert, the man of the unfinished. Whereas for me, he told himself, it's over once and for all. And there's nothing triumphant about the finale.

He started finding allusions in every note. What if the E minor weren't only Emma but himself, Michel?* He called this piece *Fuga misteriosa.* He savored in advance the moment when he'd play it for her, she who would not know the allusions and could not understand. Understand, no, but feel perhaps.

And if she didn't come back?

Emma, the note E, mi. In his madness Schumann only heard one note, A, the only vowel in Clara's name.

When Edith and Grégoire, Emma's older siblings, got married, he gave each of them a porcelain dinner service. Would he have to buy a third?

Reading the newspaper, he stumbled upon a sentence from Rivarol quoted by a columnist:

"You have to have loved very little indeed to remain friends after you've loved a great deal."

He wanted to copy this sentence and send it to Emma. Then he realized he was mad. Was this a thing to send to one's great-niece?

One winter day when she stopped by after having given a recital in Venice, she told him, "All I saw in Venice was a carousel of wooden horses on the Riva dei Schiavoni. It was foggy, so that when it turned, its red, green, blue, yellow lights made a blurred circle, unreal. It seemed like this carousel emerged from the thickness of time, from the fair in Pau when you used to take me there in November."

For once in this world without justice, where it is vain to expect the wages of good and evil, or that you might get back the love you give, Michel felt rewarded.

---

*In French musical notation, the note E is called "mi"—"E" for Emma and "mi" for Michel. *Trans.*

17

 When he came out of the métro at the Place du Châtelet, he had a moment's hesitation. Right or left? No, the Théâtre de la Ville, formerly the Sarah Bernhardt, was indeed to the right. Facing it was the Châtelet. His mother used to tell often—it was one of her most vivid childhood memories—how she had seen *Around the World in Eighty Days* there. To her enormous stupefaction, a locomotive dragged a few cars across the stage from stage right to stage left, as though it were completely natural. Travelers jumped out of the train, sat at the station buffet, ordered coffee. They were barely served when the station commander blew the whistle for departure. Everyone got back on the train. The locomotive started up, sputtering a jet of steam. The phlegmatic waiter at the buffet poured the untouched coffee back into the pot. His way of paying himself in advance. This swindle seemed to have astonished the little girl even more than the locomotive on the stage.

Michel turned his back on the Châtelet and on Geneviève's memories. Like her they weighed so little. And yet they couldn't be forgotten. At the slightest provocation, they came back in all their freshness. At the Théâtre de la Ville, he took an orchestra seat for the Atlanta Ballet, James Warner's.

He had come to Paris to negotiate the release of Nicolau Arderiu's complete works with a music publisher. Florence had finally agreed. He had chosen a moment when Emma wasn't there. She was giving a series of concerts in England and Scotland. One might have thought he was afraid to see where she lived, as if he were going to discover a place rendered unmentionable by the presence of one of those impossible companions she seemed to choose not for themselves, but to remain faithful to a type of unhappiness from which she had made the fabric of her life.

On a billboard at a street corner, James Warner's name had jumped out at him. Is that my James Warner? he had wondered. The name was so common. In the old days he always used to talk about theater and ballet, so there was some chance . . .

He was reassured when he opened the program. A brief biographical note confirmed that the famous American choreographer had spent his youth in France, in the Pyrenees.

During the performance, Virgil Thomson's music mostly bored him. As for the choreography, it was doubtless the result of a remarkable creative imagination and a very meticulous work of fine-tuning, but he knew nothing about dance, and so he observed the gestures, the movements of the ensemble, the colors of the costumes and scenery with a sort of indifference. He told himself: modern dance is jumping. And also they roll on the ground. Then he made fun of himself. I'm still in the era of *Coppélia,* the way it was danced at the Winter Palace in Pau. Soon he was only waiting for one thing, the end of the performance.

Contrary to its effect on him, the Atlanta Ballet carried the day. When the curtain fell, there was much applause, many curtain calls. This was the moment when his impatience reached its zenith. When the public stood up and started to leave the theater, when his neighbors cleared out of his row, he hastened backstage. He wandered around a minute, asked where the choreographer was, and finally found him.

It was James and it wasn't he. He saw a fat man—no, not fat, obese. In his moon face the fat formed a sort of halo that, from the double chin to the cheeks, surrounded the old face, which remained intact, the face of the student at Park Lodge. Muttering, he said, "James, my old Jimmy."

The obese man seemed to be coming out of a dream and pronounced his name: "Michel."

And he started to cry.

"You've become a great choreographer."

"What I've become . . . You see what I've become!"

Finding nothing to say, Michel began telling stories aimlessly.

"Did you know they say that the prompt box at this theater corresponds to the exact spot where Gérard de Nerval hung himself?"

The two friends went for a drink on the square. The time it takes to drink a beer isn't long enough to sum up an entire life and just suffices to sum up unhappiness, since where unhappiness is concerned, it isn't worth going into detail — a hint is all it takes.

"It was following a car accident that I started to get fat. Apparently certain glands were wrecked."

Michel asked for news of Daisy.

"She's been married twice and twice widowed, so she's rich. She lives in Europe, in Montreux on the banks of Lake Geneva. She's even more stupid than before. She's become completely conventional, respectable. She says I'm lost. In fact, I am lost, but not the way she thinks."

"I remember when you drew me the shape of her breasts," Michel said to lighten the tone.

James had forgotten.

"Does she have children?"

"No children. The Warner race will be extinguished with us. And you?"

"I don't, but my brother has a girl who had three children. The last one is a wonder. She was my pupil. Emma Dufresne. Perhaps you've heard of her."

"That young pianist with a white strand of hair."

"My great-niece, can you believe it!"

Michel explained the reason for his trip to Paris, to try to get the piano works of Nicolau Arderiu published. But their former teacher hadn't made a very strong mark on James Warner.

"Arderiu! What a phenomenon!"

That was all he said. Michel added, "He used to say you should play two roles: serious in art and not serious in life. He didn't see that in life seriousness catches up with you sooner or later. For him it was sooner."

Michel also told the story of the music Arderiu had composed for his own funeral and which had become a pop hit. He added out of pure masochism, "It's high time I wrote a little melody for my own funeral. Afterward you can make a ballet out of it."

James Warner upped the ante. "I read something good about death. By a philosopher, I don't know who or where. Probably in a magazine. If only I could get my hands on it, it would help me consider dying natural."

The American asked when they could see each other again. Michel replied that unfortunately he had to leave the next day. James nudged him: "Our reunion did me good."

"And your art, all the same, you have your art."

"Your art . . . You ought to say your art and your lard — l'art et lard! The most pathetic pun I can make in French, but it's all I'm good for. You wonder how someone as fat as I am can render those dancers light as air. It's my revenge against heaviness."

Michel wanted to respond that at least James had managed to become a great choreographer, whereas he . . . But what came out of his mouth was a turn of phrase he had been mulling over for years: "It's a relief to be a failure."

James seemed not to hear him. He was pursuing his own idea.

"Heaviness . . . In fact, Arderiu said something about that. He told me he saw Nijinsky dance. And that he had understood his secret. Nijinsky jumped, the audience held its breath, but he didn't land when you thought he would. Only a fraction of a second later. That fraction of a second, now that was his secret. Arderiu called it escaping the pull of gravity. In music as in dance, you have to escape the pull of gravity to create something new."

"I remember now," Michel said. "When he got angry because I was keeping my foot on the pedal, he used that turn of phrase. But it was especially in life that he made an effort to escape—I don't know whether it was from the pull of gravity—but in any case to escape. And I, I've tried to imitate him but awkwardly."

He started to recount what his life had been, or at least how he saw it. Florence, whom he thought he loved because after his teacher's death they were like two shipwrecked souls clinging to each other. The illusion that dissipates. His escape with Marie-Christine, another way to replay the Arderiu myth. And when finally he thought he was living for himself, the disastrous maneuvering between Pauline and Monique, one too high, the other too low for him. No, it was indecent to put it that way. Better to say: the one inaccessible and the other whom he hadn't had the courage to rescue from the depths. And there had come a moment when he had ceased to believe in the possibility of love, even as he thought more every day that without loving and being loved, we're like a fish who's been thrown up on the grass along the riverbanks.

"You know Schumann's Sonata no. 1 in F-sharp Minor? I play it often. The themes, the ideas, the images rise up endlessly beneath my fingers, and I think about my disjointed life, its jumps, its breaks."

The succession of notes, each a little world in and of itself, make up a melody. Just as the succession of events should give its legato, its meaning to life. But there comes a moment when all the episodes detach from one another like a necklace come unstrung, and one understands one hasn't had any life, any past, any history.

Music! He had lacked the courage. After the war he should have launched himself, fought. He closed himself off in his province, in his work as a teacher. He composed, yes, but for his drawers. In the end there had been Emma. Every day still he thought of her. He had given her everything he could. But he hadn't formed her for himself. It was for her, to allow her to take flight.

"No way in the world would I want her to be with me the way I was with Nicolau Arderiu. So dependent! Lucky for me he abandoned me when he took off with Florence!"

He wasn't afraid for Emma. She had come so far already.

"And little by little, I'm managing to detach myself from her."

"And afterward, what will you have left?"

He didn't dare say, "She gave me a dog."

"A reassuring idea is that I might be dead before I've completely forgotten her."

James chuckled and gave his friend a nudge.

"So, my old man, you might say we're rather desperate."

"What else can you expect? The error in life is that there always comes a moment when one believes in it."

Both of them were staying in hotels on the Left Bank. They walked part of the way together along the Pont au Change, the Quai de l'Horloge, the Pont-Neuf. It was December, but it wasn't cold yet. Michel heard in his head a fragment from one of Tchaikovsky's barcaroles that went along with the rhythm of their footsteps. They said their farewells at the corner of the Rue Bonaparte and the Rue Jacob.